Praise for the uplifting novels o

I KNOW I'V

"Grabs you from the firs
of the best reads of the y

LET THE CHURCH SAY AMEN

One of *Library Journal*'s Best Christian Books for 2004

"Billingsley infuses her text with just the right dose of humor to balance the novel's serious events. . . . Will appeal to fans of Michele Andrea Bowen's *Second Sunday* and Pat G'Orge-Walker's *Sister Betty! God's Calling You Again!*"
—*Library Journal* (starred review)

"Her community of very human saints will win readers over with their humor and verve." —*Booklist*

"Emotionally compelling. . . . Full of palpable joy, grief, and soulful characters." —*The Jacksonville Free Press*

"Amen to *Let the Church Say Amen*. . . . [A] well-written novel." —*Indianapolis Recorder*

MY BROTHER'S KEEPER

"This is a keeper." —*The Daily Oklahoman*

"Poignant, captivating, emotional, and intriguing. . . . A humorous and heart-wrenching look at how deep childhood issues can run." —*The Mississippi Link*

Also by ReShonda Tate Billingsley

Nothing But Drama
I Know I've Been Changed
Let the Church Say Amen
My Brother's Keeper
Have a Little Faith
(with Jacquelin Thomas, Sandra Kitt, and J. D. Mason)

Blessings in Disguise

ReShonda Tate Billingsley

Pocket Books
New York London Toronto Sydney

POCKET BOOKS, a division of Simon & Schuster, Inc.
1230 Avenue of the Americas, New York, NY 10020

This book is a work of fiction. Names, characters, places and incidents are products of the author's imagination or are used fictitiously. Any resemblance to actual events or locales or persons, living or dead, is entirely coincidental.

ISBN-13: 978-1-4165-2561-5
ISBN-10: 1-4165-2561-0

This Pocket Books trade paperback edition January 2007

10 9 8 7 6 5 4 3 2 1

POCKET and colophon are registered trademarks of Simon & Schuster, Inc.

Manufactured in the United States of America

For information regarding special discounts for bulk purchases, please contact Simon & Schuster Special Sales at 1-800-456-6798 or business@simonandschuster.com

For Tilly
An angel whose wings were clipped too soon
Your giving heart . . . your warm smile
lives on

Acknowledgments

So often we take for granted the gifts that God has given us. He's blessed me with the ability to tell stories that touch people's lives. So for that I give thanks. And for continuing to bless me even when I get too busy to say thanks, know that I am eternally grateful.

For those who follow my works, I know these acknowledgments get repetitive, but when you're surrounded by such wonderful and supportive people like I am, you have to thank them every chance you get. So here goes again . . .

My loving husband, whose faith in me never waivered. Thank you for loving me.

Two of the most important people in my life, my girls—Mya and Morgan. Right now, you know Mommy's books when you see them. I can't wait until you're old enough to read them. You are the motivation behind everything I do.

Mother . . . you have kept me laughing, wiped my tears, pushed me, and encouraged me to slow down. I know I don't say it enough, but thank you.

Tanisha . . . if I had to ask God to send me the perfect sister, I would ask for you. Thank you for all that you do for me.

As usual, much love to my editors, Selena James and Brigitte Smith, and my agent, Sara Camilli, for nurturing my literary career. Thank you also to Louis Burke, Melissa Gramstad, and all the other wonderful people at Simon & Schuster/Pocket Books.

To my partners in this literary game: My dear friend, Pat Tucker Wilson. We've forged a friendship that will last a lifetime. Jihad, thanks for listening to all my harebrained ideas. Eric Pete, who always makes sure I'm just "doing okay." Thanks to all the other authors who continually lift a sister up or simply offer words of wisdom: Victoria Christopher Murray, Norma Jarrett, Victor McGlothin, Nina Fox, James Guittard, Sheila Dansby Harvey, Vanessa O'Neal, and Zane and the Strebor family.

Thanks so much, as always, to the wonderful women of Alpha Kappa Alpha Sorority, Inc., especially the Houston Area Chapters, including my own—Mu Kappa Omega.

Thanks to all my family, friends, coworkers, and church members. (How do you like that? Now no one can get mad.)

But my biggest thanks goes out to you, the readers who have brought me where I am today. Thanks for showing me so much love. Drop me a line and let me know what you think of the books.

Thanks for the love.

Peace.

Blessings in Disguise

1

It oughta be a crime for somebody to talk so much.

"I mean, can you believe she had on panty hose with sandals? She looked like a country bumpkin." Trina rambled on like she was in a marathon talking contest.

I needed to get away from this girl before I killed her. Or myself. Well, not literally. But trust me when I say the way that Trina King was working my nerves, I sure thought about it.

"Aren't you glad you came to the mall with us?" Trina said, in that high-pitched Daffy Duck voice of hers.

I glared at her but didn't say anything. Shoot, I was still trying to figure out how I ended up at the mall with Alexis and her bourgie friend, Trina. If you looked up the word *Trina* in the dictionary, they'd probably have *annoying* next to it. Because that girl was the most annoying person I'd ever met.

"What, cat got your tongue?" Trina laughed like that cornball stuff was even funny. When I didn't laugh with her she turned toward Alexis. "Where did you find this sourpuss?"

Alexis laughed. "I told you, that's just how Jasmine is." She playfully hit my arm. I rolled my eyes.

Trina turned to say something to me again. I shot her a look to say don't bother.

I didn't even think it was the fact that Trina thought she was all that that made me sick. I think it was that high-pitched Daffy Duck voice and the way she was always swinging her long "top-of-the-line weave," as she called it, back and forth. Horsehair was horsehair, but she swore hers was imported from India so that made her special or something. I didn't think so.

"I think she's just jealous because we've been friends for so long," Trina said as she put her arm through Alexis's. "She doesn't want anyone messing up y'all little Good Girlz circle. But tell her, Alexis. We've been friends since junior high school. She can't compete with that."

Trina flashed a wide smile. I wanted to tell her that nobody was trying to compete with her funky behind. And no, I didn't like her being in the Good Girlz, but it wasn't like I had a choice. Trina had joined the Good Girlz a month ago after getting into some trouble at her school. Like the rest of us, she had come reluctantly. After all, the Good Girlz was a community service group for teens who had been in minor trouble. The group was sponsored by a Houston-area church called Zion Hill. Even though none of us really wanted to be in the group in the beginning, we'd come to love it. And now, it looked like Trina had, too.

"Jazzy, don't get all sensitive on me," Trina playfully said. "I'm just playing with you, girl."

I still couldn't do anything but look at her crazy. I knew I was probably being a butthole, but try as I might, I just couldn't click with that girl. Neither could Camille or

Angel, the other original members of the group. Trina was rich and uppity. Alexis was a little bit, too, but I had gotten used to Alexis. She'd rubbed me the wrong way when we first met a year ago. But now that I knew her, I just ignored her bourgie comments because I knew she had a good heart.

Trina, on the other hand, could work a nerve!

"Jazzy-Jo, why you all quiet?" Trina asked me as we made our way into yet another department store. She swung her hair back as she sashayed her tiny frame into the store.

"For the one-trillionth time, my name is Jasmine Jones. Not Jaz, not Jazzy, not Jazzy-Jo. Just Jasmine, a'ight?" I rolled my eyes and stuffed my hands in my pockets as I followed her and Alexis inside.

Trina stopped and turned toward me. "Dang, girl. Chill. Why are you such a grouch?"

Alexis smiled at me. "Jasmine is always a grouch," she said playfully.

"Whatever," I replied.

"Well, if you gon' be walking around here acting all funny, why'd you even bother to come?" Trina said.

I stared at Trina. Why *had* I come? While I liked Alexis, as soon as she said Trina was with her I should've said forget it. But my brothers were driving me insane; I was just about to hurt the youngest one when Alexis called and asked if I wanted to go to the mall. I'd seen it as the lesser of two evils.

I sighed. "I'm not being a grouch. But we've been at the mall for two hours and we haven't bought anything. Or y'all haven't bought anything, 'cause you know I ain't got no money today." Shoot, who was I kidding? I never had any money. My family put the *po* in *poor.* I couldn't tell you the last time I went shopping.

"Oh, chill out," Trina said as she made her way out of the store and into another one. "We're window-shopping, right, Alexis?"

Alexis looked uncomfortable for a minute. But she quickly snapped out of it and said, "Right. Window-shopping."

I ignored the funny look and followed them both into the store. I was surprised when they didn't start in on me about buying some new clothes. They were always trying to make me over. They claimed I looked like a tomboy because I was almost six feet tall, wore warm-ups all the time, and didn't see any purpose in makeup.

After ten minutes, I leaned against the wall and took in the sights while Trina and Alexis browsed around. Right about now I wished Camille and Angel were around. They'd at least keep me company. I people-watched for several more minutes before looking around for Alexis and Trina. I spotted them coming out of the dressing room.

"Are you all ready to go?" I asked.

"Yeah, I'm done," Trina and Alexis said in unison.

We hurried out of the store, then out of the mall. We had barely closed the doors on the car when both of them busted out laughing.

"Oh my God!" Alexis exclaimed. "That was too easy."

"I told you," Trina said. "Piece of cake."

I was sitting in the backseat and had no idea what they were talking about. "What was a piece of cake?" I asked, leaning up in the seat.

Trina looked all sneaky and stuff. "This," she said as she pulled clothes out from under her shirt.

My eyes almost jumped out of their sockets. Trina was holding up three pink Baby Phat T-shirts, all with the price tags still hanging on them.

"Trina, tell me you did not steal those," I said.

Trina smiled. "Okay, I won't tell you, then." She tossed the shirts at Alexis and turned around and started up the car.

I looked at Alexis, waiting to see the shock register on her face as well. Instead, she held the shirt up to her chest and said, "Girl, I'm going to look cute in this."

"I can't believe this," I said as I stared at the T-shirts.

"What? Girl, I got one for you," Trina said.

I looked at Trina like she'd lost her mind. "You are insane." I turned back to Alexis. "And you knew about this? You know my grandma is crazy. You trying to get me killed?"

"What's the big deal? We didn't get caught," Alexis said as Trina navigated onto the freeway. This really shocked me because the Alexis I'd come to know over the last year was sweet and straitlaced. Forget the fact that her family was loaded, stealing was just something I never thought she'd be down with.

"Plus, Alexis didn't take them. I did," Trina added, pulling me out of my thoughts. "She's too good to take things without paying for them anymore," she joked.

Anymore? I couldn't believe my ears. Judging from the designer jeans, top, and rhinestone belt that Trina had on, she could have bought plenty of T-shirts. And God knew Alexis could've bought the whole dang factory. I mean, her daddy owned a hotel and everybody knew he was loaded.

"Alexis, this is totally crazy," I said. "You have money. You have it made. And you gon' put my life in jeopardy? We could go to jail, and for what? Some stupid T-shirts?"

"You can go to jail for jaywalking but people still do it," Trina said as she switched lanes.

Alexis shrugged. "Don't worry about it. The stores have insurance. They're covered. Plus, they overcharge for this stuff anyway."

I sat back in my seat, dumbfounded. Don't get me wrong. I'm from the hood. I know some thieves. But they're hood rats, or people who steal to survive, or they steal to feed their kids. Alexis and Trina had to be the richest girls I'd ever met in my life. Their stealing made no sense to me.

Alexis turned around to face me in the backseat. "Jasmine, it's really no big . . . oh my God!" Alexis said with a look of horror across her face as she stared out of the back window. I turned to see what she was looking at.

I swear I thought I was going to pass out when I saw the flashing lights pull up behind us. Trina looked back, too, then seemed to quickly lose that confidence she'd had just a minute ago.

"I cannot believe you two are so stupid," I hissed as I turned back around and folded my arms across my chest.

"Shut up," Trina said, suddenly looking all nervous. She pulled the car over.

Alexis didn't say anything. She just sat in the front seat with a terrified look across her face.

The officer walked up to the car. "Evening, ladies. License and registration, please."

I think that had to be the closest I'd ever come to peeing on myself.

"Hello, Officer. Do you mind telling me what I was doing wrong?" Trina said with a fake smile as she reached into the glove compartment.

"I think you know what you did," the officer said.

I wanted to throw myself on his mercy and tell him I had nothing to do with the theft. I wanted to cry and beg him not to take me to jail. I just knew it was all over. They were going to throw me in a cell with someone named Big Sexy. Maybe I'd get lucky and get a cell with my cousin, Shanae, who was in jail for stabbing her husband's girlfriend. Shanae would watch my back. Oh, who was I kidding? I wasn't ready to go to jail. Everyone thought I was hard, but I'd just learned to keep my guard up because people were always giving me a hard time.

"You were going eighty in a sixty-mile-an-hour zone."

The police officer's words snapped me out of my thoughts. He took the papers Trina handed him.

I don't know about Trina and Alexis, but I wanted to turn backflips when he said that. He was stopping us for speeding.

"I am so sorry," Trina purred. "I didn't realize I was going that fast."

"Well, you were," the officer said as he looked over her insurance and registration. After a minute, he looked back up. "I see you're a 100 Club member," he said, pointing to the police support organization sticker on the back of her car.

Trina's smile grew wider. "Actually, my father is one of your biggest supporters."

The officer smiled. "Yeah, the 100 Club is a great organization. They help a lot of officers who have been hurt in the line of duty."

"I definitely agree."

It was a good thing the officer was wearing boots because Trina was shoveling it out good.

"Well, Miss King," the officer said, handing her back her license and registration. "You slow it down now, you hear?"

Trina took her stuff and smiled again. "Thank you, Officer."

I think we all held our breath until he got back to his car.

"You'd better be glad I don't carry a gun, because I would shoot you in the head right now," I growled to Trina.

"You are so violent, Jasmine." She laughed.

I sat up in the seat. "Ain't nothing funny," I said. "Do you know how close we came to going to jail? And for what, some freakin' T-shirts?"

Trina looked at me in the rearview mirror. "Stop being a Goody Two-shoes. It's just clothes. Besides, we thought you'd want in."

I looked at her like she was crazy. "Well, you thought wrong."

Trina just laughed as she pulled back into traffic. "Oh, well, more money for us," she told Alexis.

I looked at Alexis. "What is she talking about, more money?"

Alexis bit down on her lip like she didn't know what to say.

"Darling," Trina said in her best British accent, "we're

about to open shop, selling the latest fashions at prices the competition just can't beat. And we're about to get paid!"

She high-fived Alexis while I continued to sit in the backseat with my mouth hanging open. Just what their little entrepreneurial plan entailed, I didn't even want to know.

2

I was the first to arrive to tonight's Good Girlz meeting. I couldn't wait for Angel and Camille to get here so I could tell them about Alexis and Trina.

I had wanted to call them over the weekend, but since our phone was cut off until the fifteenth, that wasn't possible. Just another reason why I wished I had a cell phone. It seemed like our phone got cut off every other month. And when it was working, my oldest sister Nikki was always on it. So I'd asked for a cell phone for my birthday. My grandmother had almost choked from laughter.

I paced back and forth across the meeting room, wishing they'd hurry up. Angel and Camille usually came to the meetings together. I was just about to go wait in the parking lot when both of them came bouncing into the room.

"What took y'all so long?" I asked.

"Huh?" Angel said. "What time is it?"

Camille looked at her watch. "It's only 6:30. We're not late. What are you talking about?"

I blew out a frustrated breath, peeked down the hall, then shut the door.

"What is wrong with you?" Camille asked.

"Yeah, and why are you here so early? You're always the last to arrive," Angel added.

"You two are not going to believe this," I said.

"What?" both of them said at the same time.

"I went to the mall with Alexis and Trina this weekend," I began.

"You're right," Camille interrupted. "I don't believe you, of all people, were hanging with Alexis and Trina. And at the mall nonetheless." Both Camille and Angel started laughing.

"Would you two stop cracking jokes? This is serious," I chastised.

They could both see I wasn't kidding because the smiles left their faces. Since I had their undivided attention, I continued. "When we left the mall and got back to the car, Trina pulled clothes out of her shirt, clothes she had stolen from the mall."

"You are lying," Camille said, her eyes wide.

"If I'm lying, I'm flying," I responded.

"Alexis doesn't steal. She doesn't need to," Angel said, as if the idea itself was absurd.

"That's the same thing I said. She didn't actually take anything but she knew what Trina was doing." I leaned in and lowered my voice. "I think they've been doing it awhile. And get this—I think they may be getting ready to sell the stuff."

"Jasmine, you must've misunderstood—" Camille stopped mid-sentence and all of us turned toward the door as it slowly opened.

"Hey, everybody. What's up?" Alexis said as she walked in. All three of us stared at her as she walked in and dropped her Gucci purse in a chair.

I looked at Alexis, unsure of what I should say. She must've read the look on my face because she crossed her arms across her chest and rolled her eyes. "I guess you told them."

"You guessed right," I replied. All four of us had grown tight over the past year so Alexis had to know that I was going to tell Camille and Angel.

"So? It's no big deal anyway," Alexis said as she took a seat.

"So it's true?" Angel said, walking over to Alexis.

"It's not as serious as I'm sure Jasmine made it out to be." Alexis cut her eyes at me.

"Alexis, what's going on?" Camille said, sitting down next to her.

Alexis broke out into a huge smile. "Trina and I have this cool business going on. She and her cousin get the stuff and then we sell it out of my house."

"So you *are* selling the stuff?" I threw my hands up in disgust. "That's just great."

Alexis ignored me and looked at Camille. "See, the stores all have insurance that replaces the lost stuff so it's not like it's hurting them."

Before Camille could respond, our group leader, Rachel Adams, walked in. She was the first lady of Zion Hill and the founder of Good Girlz. The room grew silent when she entered.

"Don't stop talking on my account," Rachel said as she eyed all of us suspiciously. "You all want to tell me what you're talking about that you don't want me to know?"

We looked at one another. Part of me really wanted to tell Rachel what we were talking about. Maybe she could talk some sense into Alexis. But, of course, I didn't want to sell out my friend like that.

"We were just discussing community service project ideas," Alexis said. I stared at her. I couldn't believe she was sitting up in church lying to the first lady.

Rachel gave us a sly smile as she walked to the front of the room. "Sure you were. But since you say you're on the subject of community service projects, let's hear some of them."

I sat down as well. We spent the next hour going over ideas but my mind was everywhere but in that room. I knew I was wrong, but I sure was glad when Rachel started praying because that meant we were about to wrap up the meeting. I was anxious to talk some sense into these girls. They were from these prissy worlds and just didn't understand the kind of trouble they were setting themselves up for.

After Rachel dismissed us, Alexis dang near broke her neck trying to get outside. I caught up with her at the car, where she was leaning over whispering to Camille and Angel.

"Okay, Trina wants to meet us at my house at nine. She had to go to the wake of a great aunt, that's why she's not here tonight. But she still wanted us to get together tonight so we could open for business tomorrow because the Ladies of Distinction are having a slumber party and they've all promised to come by." Alexis talked like she was brokering some million-dollar deal. I stood just outside their little circle with my arms crossed.

"What?" Alexis said when she finally noticed me. "Don't start, Jasmine."

"I just can't believe you," I said. "I mean, how did you even get caught up in something like this?"

"For your information, Miss Goody Two-shoes, Trina's cousin hooked her up, then she had me just helping her out. It's not that serious."

"If you get the stuff from her cousin, why y'all out lifting stuff?" I asked.

"What, are you the police now?" Alexis replied. I knew she was getting agitated but I didn't care. "Fine," she huffed. "If you must know, we don't usually take the stuff ourselves. Trina just started getting some special requests for outfits, so she came up with the idea to open our own little business and pick up some stuff ourselves. Is that answer good enough for you?"

I couldn't do anything but shake my head.

"Dang, Jasmine. You act like we're taking stuff from you," Alexis said. Finally, she threw her hands up and turned back to Camille.

"You still coming?" Alexis said.

Camille was standing there looking all bug-eyed. It was obvious both she and Angel were excited. "What kind of stuff do you have?" Camille wanted to know.

"Trina got some of everything, girl."

"So, she just walks in and takes the stuff off the rack?" Angel whispered.

"Let's not get into how she got it. All that matters is she got it. Now, if you all want in, let me know."

"Oh, I can't steal anything. Angelica needs me and I can't take the risk of going to jail," Angel said, referring to her six-month-old baby girl.

"And you know I did a week in juvie. Me and jail don't get along," Camille added.

I couldn't believe Camille was even thinking about anything that could get her in trouble. After her boyfriend broke out of jail, didn't tell her he broke out, and convinced her to hide him at her grandmother's house, she'd been arrested. Camille almost lost her mind, but the judge told her she didn't have to go to jail as long as she took part in the Good Girlz group.

"No one's going to jail," Alexis said, rolling her eyes at me. "For some reason Trina gets off on taking the stuff. And she only does that occasionally. Her cousin usually gets all the stuff. All she wants us to do is get the customers in and store the merchandise because her mother is so nosy."

"Is that all she wants?" I snapped. "Alexis, this is crazy. You're freakin' loaded. Why are you doing this?"

Alexis ignored me and kept talking. "Camille, why don't you guys just come by and check it out? If you're game, you can help us sort the stuff. And hey, maybe even pick up a thing or two for yourselves."

Angel pulled up Camille's arm and looked at her watch. "I really have to be getting home. My mom is with Angelica and she has to go to work at ten."

"How's your mom with the baby?" Alexis asked.

I knew she was trying to get attention off of herself by asking about Angel's relationship with her mom, which had been shaky because Angel had gotten pregnant at fifteen.

"Nah, she's cool now," Angel said. "She's really come around and she loves Angelica. But she was serious when she said I wasn't gon' run the streets. She totally trips if I leave Angelica with her too long."

"I bet she'd trip even more if she knew you were off stealing clothes," I said, shaking my head.

"I'm not even trying to hear you," Alexis said as she turned to Camille. "Are you coming or not?"

"Hey, why not?" Camille shrugged.

I looked at her. "I don't believe you."

"I'm just going to look and see what kind of stuff they got," she responded.

"Whatever." I threw my hands up just as my grandmother pulled into the parking lot. "Just let me know when visiting days are." I shook my head as I climbed in my grandmother's car. I could see they were gon' have to learn the hard way.

3

"Jasminium Nichelle Solé Jones! If you don't get your tail in this kitchen, you will live to regret it!"

I absolutely, positively hated my name. I couldn't for the life of me understand why my mother would give me such a dumb and long name. I hated it even worse when people used the whole thing. And I especially couldn't stand it when my mother screamed it the way she was doing right now.

Maybe if I don't answer her, she'll go away. I rolled over and turned up the volume to BET, which was showing the new Usher video. I was just grateful to have the TV to myself for a change. Everybody except my mother was gone to church. I had acted like I was sick and even then my grandmother didn't want me to stay home, talking 'bout "the Lord will heal what ails me."

I hated my life. I couldn't stand my mean brothers and my lazy sister. My grandmother got on my nerves, too. Mostly because she slept in the same room with me and snored so loud that it kept me up most nights. But my mom drove me the craziest. I knew she thought I didn't appreciate how hard she works for us, but I did. It was just that she works my nerves, always griping and fussing about something.

My family just didn't get how hard it was being me. Even though I was a middle child, you'd never know it because it seemed like everything was my responsibility. Nikki, who was two years older than me, worked part-time and used that little job at the beauty supply store as an excuse to get out of doing any chores.

My mother worked two jobs—as a housekeeper at the Westin Hotel and as a security guard—so she was never here to help out. And my grandmother had arthritis so bad, she could hardly do anything. So everything basically fell on my shoulders.

I was nothing but a glorified maid. Shoot, scrap that, I wasn't even glorified. I was just a maid.

I sighed as I watched Usher dance across the TV screen. He reminded me of C.J. I couldn't stop thinking about the fact that the only boy I had ever remotely been interested in had called me Grape Ape at school on Friday. I had thought about punching C.J. in his jaw when he said it. And I would have if I didn't get butterflies every time I got near him.

Then on top of that, I was flunking PE.

"How do you flunk PE?" my mother had screamed. My mother screamed everything. Sometimes I wondered if she even knew how to talk in a calm, rational voice.

I had just shrugged. I didn't bother to tell her it was because I refused to change clothes. Since I was the biggest girl in the class, I didn't want to wear those dumb, skimpy little gym shorts. I'd just take my F. It wasn't like I was going to college anyway. We couldn't afford to buy one book at college, let alone pay for a whole semester's worth of tuition.

"Jasmine, do you hear me talking to you?"

I looked up. I hadn't even noticed my mother standing in the doorway to my bedroom. I really wasn't in the mood to go at it with her. I found myself wishing it was next weekend already. We were spending the night over Alexis's house and I looked forward to anything that took me away from here.

"What?" I said.

"What? Did you tell me what?" my mother yelled. She was standing there in her security guard uniform.

"Mama, I'm right here. You ain't gotta yell," I calmly said.

"Don't tell me what I ain't gotta do! This is my house. If I want to yell at the top of my lungs, I will! And you 'bout to get knocked upside the head, telling me what."

I took a deep breath. Did I mention I hated my life?

"Why is that kitchen like that?" my mother asked. "I told you before I left last night to clean that kitchen up."

"It's Nikki's turn."

"You knew Nikki was going out with Tony. That's why I told you to do it."

I wanted to scream. How could going out with a boy get you out of chores? I guess it probably had something to do with the fact that Tony was a superstar basketball player at his high school across town and everybody expected him to go pro straight out of high school. Nikki was hanging on to Tony for dear life, hoping he was her ticket out of our pitiful lifestyle. My mother let Nikki get away with murder when it came to Tony.

"So I guess all I gotta do is find me a boyfriend and I won't have to do anything around the house, either," I groaned.

"I guess you better watch that smart-aleck mouth." My mother shot me an evil look. "Why aren't you at church anyway?"

"Because I'm"—I paused to cough—"I'm sick."

"You might have fooled your grandmother with that nonsense, but I know better. I done told you about missing church."

How she even fixed her lips to say that was beyond me. Especially since she hadn't been to church in almost six months. "I went to two Good Girlz meetings at church this week so doesn't that mean that I've met my church quota for the week?"

My mother sighed heavily. "I'm tired. I've worked all night and I don't have time for your smart mouth. I'm goin' to lay down. When I get up, I betta not see them dishes in the sink. And when you're finished doing the dishes, mop the kitchen floor." She spun out the room.

I stuck my lips out and fell back on the bed. I couldn't say it enough. I hated my life.

4

It seemed as if someone had opened the floodgates in the sky. Rain was pouring down, and I was hoping it would let up because I had to catch the bus to the Good Girlz meeting this evening. I was not in the mood to get drenched.

I had just gotten in from school and was leaning in the refrigerator looking for the pizza I had saved from this weekend. I'd wrapped it up in some foil and pushed it way in the back behind the milk so no one would see it. I'd even written my name on it, along with "DO NOT EAT," with a black Magic Marker. I moved the milk and just about everything else on the top shelf. Nothing.

"Hey! Did somebody eat my pizza?" I yelled as I slammed the door shut and stomped into the living room where my three brothers were strewn across the sofa watching *Fear Factor*.

"Hey, did one of you fools eat my pizza?"

Nobody responded.

I kicked my oldest brother's foot. "Jaquan, did you hear me?"

He moved his leg, but kept his eyes on the TV. "Naw, girl. I didn't touch your pizza."

I went and stood in front of the television, my hands planted firmly on my hips. "Y'all playing dumb, but I know one of you ate my dang pizza." At that moment, I noticed the paper plate sitting on the end table. On it were three pizza crusts.

"I don't believe this!" I rushed over and picked up the plate. "I told you not to touch my stuff!" I started waving the plate around and the crust went flying to the floor. "Who ate it?"

"Wasn't me," all three said in unison.

I was burning mad. It wasn't just the fact that I was starving because I hadn't eaten lunch, but I was so sick of never being able to have anything, from food to clothes, because one of my stupid brothers or my sister was always taking my stuff.

"I hate all of you!"

"You of all people don't need pizza anyway." Jaquan laughed. My other brothers—Jaheim and Jalen—laughed along with him.

I was fed up. I lunged toward Jaquan and had him pinned to the floor before he knew what hit him. He screamed and punched with all of his might but couldn't get the upper hand.

"Have y'all done lost your minds?"

We stopped tussling and turned toward the front door. My grandmother stood there, her bulky purse slung across her shoulder. Several grocery bags filled her hands.

"I know y'all not up in my living room fighting like some hooligans," she said as she walked in and closed the door.

"Jaquan ate my pizza," I cried as I pulled myself up off the floor.

"No, I didn't."

"You did!"

"Would you two stop it! I have a headache and I don't feel like hearing all this noise." She motioned toward Jaheim. "Jaheim, come get these groceries. You see me struggling."

Both boys jumped up and took the bags from my grandmother. She breathed a sigh of relief. "Now," she said as she reached in her purse. "I didn't realize until I got home that I forgot to get some bread and some bologna." She pulled out her wallet. "Jasmine, I need you to take my EBT card and run back to the grocery store."

I looked at my grandmother like she was completely crazy. "That's a food stamp card," I said like she didn't know.

"And? It's how you eat every night, so don't go acting like you too good to use food stamps."

I just stared at the card, which my grandmother held out toward me. Tori Young from my school worked at that grocery store, which was just down the street. There was no way I was going to be seen up in there using a food stamp card. "Why can't Jaquan go?"

"Because I'm telling you to go," my grandmother said as she thrust the card toward me.

I wanted to protest some more. But I knew my grandmother. There was no reasoning with her. I reached out to grab the card and my grandmother pulled it back.

"I just know you were not about to snatch this out of my hand."

I lowered my head.

"Do you hear me talking to you?" my grandmother asked.

"Yes, ma'am. And no, I wasn't about to snatch it."

My grandmother huffed as she handed me the card. "Don't ever think you too good for something, you hear me?" she said as she stomped into the kitchen.

I looked over at my brothers. They were all sitting on the sofa trying not to laugh. "Y'all make me sick," I muttered before slipping on my flip-flops and heading out the door.

It took me less than ten minutes to walk to the store. Once there I made a mad dash to get the bread and lunch meat. As I approached the counter, I looked around to make sure I didn't see anyone I knew.

"Good," I mumbled when I didn't see Tori working at any of the registers. I walked to the register with the shortest line and stood impatiently behind a woman with two kids.

I almost died when the woman pulled out a stack of coupons. I turned to go get in another line and bumped into the cutest boy I had ever seen in my life.

"Dang, what's your hurry, girl?" the boy said as he grabbed the meat, which I'd dropped when I ran into him.

I was speechless as he handed the meat back to me. He was taller than me, which didn't happen very often. That in itself was appealing, but he had these gorgeous hazel eyes, a closely cropped cut, and a square jaw topped off a body that could put Tyrese to shame. Matter of fact, he looked like a taller, lighter version of Tyrese.

"Hello? Do you speak English," the guy said with a smile.

"Oh, umm, yeah, sorry. I was just in a hurry," I said as I took the meat.

The boy pointed to the register. "Well, you don't have to move out of this line. It looks like that lady forgot her money, so you're next."

I turned toward the woman, who looked frustrated as she dug through her purse.

"Please hold my groceries. I'll be right back," the woman said as she rushed off.

I froze. There was no way I was about to use this stupid card now.

"Well, are you going to go or what?"

Think, Jasmine, think, I kept telling myself.

"Ummm, I just remembered I forgot to get something," I said.

The boy smiled again. He had the whitest teeth. I felt goose bumps crawl up my arm. "Why don't I walk with you? Maybe I can get your name," he said.

My eyes bugged out. "Ummm, nah. I'm in a hurry."

"I can walk fast," the boy said with a grin.

"That's okay," I stuttered.

The boy shrugged, the smile still across his face. "Okay, I can take a hint."

"Well, can y'all take that dang flirting somewhere else? You holding up the line!" an old man standing behind us snapped.

The boy laughed and then stepped aside. "Sorry, Pops. Why don't you go ahead."

"I ain't your pops," the old man said as he wobbled past us with his groceries.

"Can I at least get your name?" the boy said, turning his attention back to me and pulling me out of line.

I drew a blank. He laughed. I know he must have thought I was a nutcase.

"Okay, obviously this isn't working. I'm Donovan. And you are?"

What was my name? I swear, I couldn't remember it. I couldn't remember anything at that very moment. "Jasmine," I finally said, coming out of my daze.

"Well, Jasmine, since you won't let me walk with you, will you at least give me your number so I can call you sometime?" I couldn't take my eyes off this boy. He had to be the finest boy I'd ever seen in my life.

I know I looked like a special ed student or something the way I was just standing there staring at him.

He shook his head. "Look, why don't I just give you my number and if you call, you call." He reached in his back pocket, pulled out a piece of paper and a pen, and wrote his number down.

He held the paper up in front of me and flashed those Colgate commercial–looking teeth. "I really hope you'll use this, Jasmine."

I just knew my heart was about to jump out of my chest as he leaned in and pushed the piece of paper down in the front pocket of my jeans. "You are so pretty."

Pretty? That was not something many people used to describe me. I mean, I have been told I have a pretty face, but since I was so tall and a little thick, that was usually all people saw.

"I would really like to get to know you better, Jasmine. I hope you'll call," he said. He flashed a smile one last time before turning and heading back to the register.

I was still standing there in a daze as he paid for his soda, then walked out of the front door.

5

I doubled over with laughter as I walked down the hallway. Camille had just cracked a joke about the funny-looking marlin somebody had drawn on a poster hanging in the hallway. The marlin was our school mascot here at Madison, but she said that picture looked more like Nemo.

Camille was forever cracking jokes and today was no exception. I needed to laugh because I couldn't get Donovan off of my mind. I'd been thinking about him since I met him three days ago. Of course I hadn't called, but I still couldn't stop thinking about him.

Camille had moved on from the jacked-up poster and was now talking about some nerd who tried to holla at her in her last class.

"Girl, you are too stupid," Angel said. I was happy she'd transferred to our school because we kicked it all the time now.

"For real. That boy looks just like Chicken Little," Camille said. "And then gon' . . ." Camille's words died off as she focused her attention down the hall. "Good God Almighty," she said with her eyes wide.

I followed her gaze. "Wha—" I stopped in my tracks when I saw what Camille was looking at. Donovan!

"Is he fine or what?" Camille grabbed my arm to steady herself, never taking her eyes off Donovan, who was walking toward us.

"He's coming this way," Camille whispered. I still didn't say anything but Camille didn't seem to notice because she had such a huge grin across her face. She ran her fingers through her spiral curls and stuck her chest out as Donovan approached.

He shifted his backpack and stopped right in front of us. "Well, hello," he said.

Camille started toying with one of her shoulder-length curls.

"Hi yourself," she said, shamelessly flirting.

He smiled at Camille, then turned to me. "I waited for you to call."

Camille's smile faded and a confused look crossed her face. I ignored it as I tried to force a smile myself. I had to keep it together. I couldn't make a fool out of myself again, especially in front of Camille and the other girls who had stopped in the hallway and started to stare at this new face around campus.

"Ummm, I was going to," I said, trying to remember what Camille told me about being more girlie. My friends were always after me to act more like a "young lady," as Alexis always says.

"You just hadn't gotten around to it yet, right? Even though it's been three days." He smiled. I blushed.

"It's cool. You're worth waiting for." He reached up and gently squeezed my arm. "See you around, pretty lady." He continued walking down the hall.

Neither me, nor Camille, nor the group of girls standing nearby at a locker, took our eyes from him as he walked off. When he turned the corner, I turned to Camille, who had a look of shock on her face.

"What?" I said, trying to act like it was no big deal. "Close your mouth," I snapped when she didn't say anything.

Camille shook her head. "Okay, I know that was game he was running, but he is so fine, it doesn't even matter."

I laughed, then looked at my watch, trying not to let my excitement show. "We better get going before we're late for our next class."

"Oh, no you don't," Camille said as she moved to block me from walking away. "You're just gon' have to take a tardy because you're not going anywhere until you tell me who that is and how you know him."

I just shrugged. My stomach was turning backflips, but I didn't want Camille to know that. "He's just a guy I met." Camille was the boy-crazy one. I didn't want anyone to think I was all worked up over some dude.

"That fine thing I just saw is not 'just some guy.' "

I smiled, no longer able to contain my excitement. "He is fine, ain't he?"

"And then some." Camille looked down the hall to where he'd disappeared."He's got to be new here." She turned back to me. "And what did he mean, he waited on you to call?"

"Just what he said," I said as we started walking down the hall again.

"You have his number? What's his name? How'd you meet him?"

"What is this, twenty questions?" I quipped.

"And you haven't answered a single one of them."

I stopped and turned to Camille. "His name is Donovan. I met him in the grocery store on Monday. He gave me his number and asked me to call him."

"And you haven't called him yet? It's Thursday," Camille said like she couldn't even fathom the idea.

"Nope."

"What are you waiting on? Is he new here?"

"I don't know anything about him. And I don't know, I just didn't get around to calling."

"Girl, you're better than me, because I would've called him as soon as I got in the house the day we met."

"That's because you're boy-crazy."

"Whatever. So you're calling him tonight, right?"

I shrugged. "I don't know. I mean, come on, that boy is all that. I don't even need to waste my time."

"And why is that? He obviously likes you. I mean, dang, I saw the way he looked at you. He didn't even glance my way."

"Stop exaggerating." I wished that were true. I had never had a boyfriend. I used to like C.J. when I first started going to Madison. But he turned out to be a jerk. "Guys like that do not go for girls like me."

"So why would he give you his number then?"

"Because that's what guys like him do," I stated matter-of-factly.

We had finally reached my Algebra class. Camille stopped me just as I was about to walk inside. "Jasmine, you've said a lot of dumb stuff since I met you. But thinking he's too good for you is the dumbest. You better call that boy. Did you see how Tori and 'nem were looking at him? He's gotta be new and I guarantee you, by the end of the week, every girl in school is going to be trying to get with him," she said with a serious expression on her face.

"That's just it, Camille. I'm not about to be fighting every girl up in this school over a boy," I replied, just as serious.

"Have you ever thought that you might not have to fight? Not if it's you that he wants. Think about what I'm saying." Camille strutted off as I replayed her words over and over in my head.

6

I know Miss Rachel could tell I wasn't into the meeting, but I had been in a funk all day long.

After I saw Donovan yesterday, I broke down and called him when I got home. Our conversation was going so well until Jaquan picked up the other phone and yelled that my grandmother wanted me to come fold up the clothes before she beat my behind. I was so embarrassed. Especially when he added, "I don't know why you talkin' to a boy no way. It ain't like you can go out on no dates."

Donovan laughed it off, but I wanted to scream. So between that, the D I made on my research paper, and me having to spend the whole afternoon cleaning the house, I was not in a good mood.

Rachel definitely noticed my mood change because her laughter died down as she looked at me. "Hey, you, what's up? You don't seem like you're here with us today."

I shrugged. "I don't know. Just in a bad mood, I guess."

"Care to talk about it?" Rachel asked.

"Not really."

"Unh-uh, Jasmine," Angel piped in. "You are the only one who hasn't really opened up. One minute you're all right, the next you're in a foul mood and nobody knows why."

"She's right," Alexis added. "You're always talking about you'll tell your story one day. Well, it's one day."

I rolled my eyes. Since we started this group, everyone had pretty much opened up to one another. Everyone except me. Camille had drama with her mama and her convict boyfriend. And Angel had gotten pregnant at fifteen. And Alexis had her drama with her parents. But none of it compared to my story. They all knew I was broke as all getout. But they didn't understand what things were like at my home. And they sure couldn't understand the burning desire I had inside to live a different life.

"You know what, you can sit there looking like Oscar the Grouch all you want. Nobody cares about that," Camille said.

"Yeah, now tell us what's wrong," Angel added.

I wanted so bad to tell them to leave me alone, but I couldn't help the heaviness that I felt in my heart. I tried to open my mouth, and suddenly tears started coming. The sight of me crying must've really freaked everyone out because they gathered around me, all bug-eyed. Everyone thought I was so hard, so seeing me snottin' all over the place must have been a scary sight.

"Oh my God, Jasmine." Alexis wrapped her arms around my neck. "What's wrong?"

Normally, I would've pushed Alexis off of me, but all I could do was cover my face with my hands and sob.

"Sweetie, talk to us. Tell us what's wrong," Rachel said softly.

"I . . . I hate it at home." I struggled to get the words

out, I was crying so hard. "I'm so sick of my life. I wish I could go live with my father."

The room grew silent. Everyone was probably shocked that I even mentioned my father. Other than telling them I had no idea where he was, I had never shared much about him or my desire to see him.

"Jasmine, are you sure you want to do that? Sometimes we have to be grateful for the things we have in our life," Rachel said. I looked up at her and saw the doubt in her eyes. She knew my home situation. Rachel used to babysit me when I was a little girl, so she knew how the subject of my father was taboo in our house.

"I just feel like I don't belong in my family. Like I'm supposed to be living a different life." I was shocking even myself. "And I can't help but wonder what my father is like. Does he have a family? Does he live in a nice house? What he looks like . . . why he left me . . . where he lives."

"Why don't you ask your mom?" Angel said.

I wiped my tears. "Yeah, right. If I even mention his name, she gets all up in a tizzy. I think his name is Frank." I sniffed. "How pathetic is that that I don't even know my father's name for sure? But I've never met him and my mother refuses to talk about him. Nikki's daddy died but she still talks to his family. My brothers have the same father and he comes to see them all the time. Me? I don't have anybody."

I don't know why I was suddenly opening up so, but everything I'd been holding inside seemed to come pouring out.

"I know my dad is alive because I heard my aunt talking about him to my mom," I continued. "But that's all I know. I've tried to ask my grandmother and she tells me to go ask my mama. I just need some answers. I want to find him."

Everyone just looked at me all pitiful for a few minutes. "I know how we can find your father," Alexis said.

I sat up and sniffed again. "For real?"

Alexis nodded. "We can use the Internet and my friend's brother, who works as a private detective, can help us out."

"Don't play, Alexis," I said, not wanting to believe finding my father was even a possibility. I was just venting. I definitely didn't think it would ever happen.

"I'm serious. You say the word and he's as good as found."

Rachel stood up like she knew she needed to be the voice of reason. "And tell me, Jasmine, what do you plan to do once you find him?"

I shrugged again. I hadn't thought that far ahead. Heck, I hadn't thought much about anything. I just knew if there was a chance of me finding my father, I had to take it. My life sucked so bad and I just had a feeling my father was what I needed to make everything all right.

7

"This place is a funky mess, Jaquan. You get your butt off that couch and clean up this living room!" I yelled.

There were empty potato chip bags, video games, and DVDs all across the floor.

"I'm sick of this. Y'all think I'm about to be cleaning up after your nasty butts? I ain't your personal maid. And whose turn is it to wash the dishes?"

My brothers drove me crazy. They were trifling, obnoxious, and lazy. Jaheim was eleven and Jalen was four. But fifteen-year-old Jaquan was the worst. He aggravated me the most and we fought like cat and dog.

Now, looking around this filthy room, I was even more disgusted. Especially because I was the one who would get in trouble if Granny came home and found the place looking like this.

"The house is a nasty pigsty!" They still weren't listening to me as they lay on the living room floor playing some stupid video game. I kicked Jaquan's leg. If these clowns didn't clean up now, I knew Granny was gonna make me do it when she got home. I couldn't believe the way they were just sitting there ignoring me, like I'd never even walked into the room.

I made my way into the kitchen. And the minute I hit the entryway I was hot. When I looked around and saw plates, pots, and glasses from the night before, I wanted to strangle those little punks.

"Now I know somebody done lost their freakin' mind! Who was supposed to do the dishes last night? Unh-unh, y'all think I'm playing around here. It ain't even going down like this," I screamed.

When those fools continued to giggle at the screen and work their game controllers as I ranted and raved, I felt like I was about to lose it.

"I don't believe you 'bout to make it to the next level. That's tight! You see that?" Jaheim yelled.

It was like they hadn't heard a word I said. I walked back into the living room and over to the wall, where I yanked the television cord out of the socket.

"What the—!"

I looked at Jaquan. "I wish you would, so I could tell Granny you cussing up in here," I dared him.

He looked at me with pure hatred in his eyes as I dangled the cord from my hand. I plastered on the most wicked smile I could muster up.

"I don't believe she did that, man. You ain't never got to that level before," Jaheim said as he shook his head.

"Ooooh, you gon' pay for that," Jaquan said through clenched teeth.

I was ready if he even thought about trying me. I twirled the cord in my hand almost daring any one of them to try me.

"Now I said, y'all gon' clean this doggone place up and I mean fast. I ain't got time to be picking up behind y'alls' trifling behinds. And somebody better get in that kitchen. I am not playing!" I crossed my arms on my chest and stood there looking at them. Jaquan hadn't moved or uttered a word.

"You feeling froggy? Jump, fool." My brother wasn't crazy. I stood a good two feet taller than him and he knew he was no match for me. I was hoping he would come at me, though, because I wanted to beat his tail. I had been dreaming about the special kind of headlock I planned to put him in the minute we got into it again. Oh, I had something waiting for him, all right, but it didn't seem like Jaquan was looking for trouble.

I didn't even hear my grandmother's keys in the door. By the time I realized she was home, Jaheim and Jalen had started picking up the mess all over the living room.

"What's going on here with you two?" my grandmother asked.

"Nothing," I said. "Jaquan just finished his video game and was just about to go and clean the kitchen like you told him to before he went to bed last night."

He shot me the evil eye, but he didn't dare say a word.

"I keep telling y'all to stop spending hours on those video games, nothing gets done around here!" my grandmother said as she placed her purse on the table.

"I keep telling them the same thing, Granny," I said in a singsong voice, twisting my neck as Jaquan sulked toward the kitchen. Now who was laughing? Not only was he mad about the game, but I knew he was even more upset about having to clean the kitchen. If I knew my brothers, they were probably playing to see who would have to clean it. So many times before they'd bet each other and the loser had to do the chores. I was usually on the losing end of those bets even though I was never a part of them. If chores stayed unfinished for too long, I was always the old reliable backup. And I had gotten tired of it a long time ago.

"Whew! I'm so tired," my grandmother said. "I'm about to go lie down for a spell. Jasmine, wake me up in about forty-five minutes. Did you clean that chicken yet?" she asked.

"No ma'am. Um, I was about to, but I couldn't because the sink was so full of dishes. And I know how you don't like it when food is near all those dirty dishes," I offered.

My grandmother looked at me and frowned. "Get in there and help your brother straighten up that kitchen. Then clean that chicken."

I lowered my head. "Yes ma'am."

She looked at Jalen and Jaheim. "And clean up this living room."

The minute I walked into the kitchen Jaquan removed his hands from the sudsy water and doused me with it. He started cracking up.

"Oh no you didn't!" I felt my hair, which had gotten wet. That was the last straw. God as my witness, I wanted to take his head and drown it under the dishwater. I walked over to the sink and stomped on his foot.

"Ooouch!" he screamed, doubling over in pain.

That was when I made my move. I quickly grabbed his head and held it in the crook of my arm. I pulled it near my chest and squeezed. He immediately started clawing toward my arm, and I tightened my grip.

"Fight! Fight! Fight!" I heard Jalen begin to sing.

"Oh, she gettin' you, Jaquan. She gettin' you, man," Jaheim said as he raced into the kitchen.

The more Jaquan squirmed and tried to break free, the tighter I held his head. I could feel him starting to sweat, but I hung on for dear life.

"Now what, you little punk? Now what?"

"You betta . . ." he managed to say, even though it was nothing more than a whisper.

"I betta what? What you gon' do now, huh? What? You not talking any more mess now I see," I challenged.

Things were going good until we bumped into the kitchen table and made a crashing noise. I lost my footing and we tumbled to the floor. He was too fast for me. Once he was free from the headlock, he climbed on me and pinned me to the floor.

"Get off of me!" I yelled.

"Oh, now what?" he said.

"Get her, man, get her," Jaheim sang.

Once he had me pinned on the floor, he used his knees to keep my arms to the floor.

"You better stop, Jaquan, I ain't playing with you!" I struggled to get up, but I couldn't. I looked up and hanging between his lips was a long line of spit.

"Eeewww, if you spit on me, I swear, I'ma kill you!" I squirmed, trying to twist and turn my head away from him. I turned to the left; he and his spit followed me. I turned to the right and he did the same. My brothers were such disgusting little freaks!

"If you spit on your sister, I'm gonna smack you into next week," my grandmother said, suddenly appearing in the doorway. "Now quit that horsing around, get up, and clean this place up! This house better be spick-and-span before you leave outta here for that meeting, Jasmine." She watched me as I struggled up off the ground. "And look at you. You ought to know better. Now, I suggest y'all get busy in here. If I gotta come back in, y'all ain't gonna like it!" she promised. She turned and stormed out of the room.

I glared at Jaquan as I grabbed a dish towel. Today confirmed it—I needed to get out of this place before I went stone crazy.

8

I couldn't believe I was standing here giggling like some little junior high girl. But that was the way I felt every time Donavan stood within an inch of me.

We were outside in the courtyard at school. It was lunchtime and people were running all over the place. But I might as well have been alone with Donovan because no one else had my attention.

"Jasmine, I'm really feeling you," Donovan said with his signature smile. "I mean, not only are you funny, pretty, and fine, but I just love your height."

I thought I had died and gone to heaven. Me funny, pretty, fine? And I dang sure hadn't ever had anybody tell me they liked my height.

"Thank you." I blushed. It was hard to believe it had only been three weeks since we met. Since we talked every day, it seemed like much longer. I was nervous as all get-out because I just knew our phone would get cut off this month. I was so glad when I heard Mama tell Granny she was broke because she paid the phone bill. The last thing I wanted was to have Donovan call me and then get a recording saying our number was disconnected.

"You know I love talkin' to you on the phone, but when are we gonna be able to go out?" he said, taking my hand.

Before I could reply, Camille and Angel walked by. "Hey, Jasmine, we missed you at lunch today," Camille said coyly.

"Yeah," Angel added. "I think this is the first time Jasmine ditched us for lunch." They both turned to Donovan. "What's up, Donovan?"

"Nothing much, ladies. How are you all doing?"

"Fine—a little sad because our girl seems to have dumped us for something better," Camille said as she looked Donovan up and down.

I gave them the evil eye, hoping they weren't about to embarrass me.

Donovan laughed as he looked at me. "Oh, am I the something better?"

I felt my throat go dry. I was getting mad at myself because I still got all flustered and stuff around him. Getting flustered behind a boy wasn't my nature, so this was coming as a shock.

Luckily, Camille came to my rescue. "Yeah, you're definitely the something better. All she talks about is 'Donovan is so cute, Donovan is so fine, Donovan is so smart,' " she said mockingly.

Now she was going a bit too far. Donovan just laughed. "That's good to know because I was starting to wonder if she was feeling me like I was feeling her."

Camille and Angel giggled. Me? I was silently willing the knots in my stomach to go away.

Donovan was just about to say something else when Tori and her group of snobby friends walked up. "Hey

Donovan," Tori said, ignoring the rest of us. "Are you getting settled at our illustrious school?" She swung her long, jet-black hair over her shoulder.

"I am," Donovan said. I was pleased that he didn't flash her a smile. Tori usually made guys smile. She was about five-foot-five and a size six, had long beautiful hair and was a beautiful chocolate color. She was also a snob who had lucked out and got voted Miss Madison, captain of the cheerleaders, and president of the honor society. I couldn't stand her.

"We're looking forward to you playing in the UIL tournament," she said, trying to sound all sexy.

"Yeah, I'm looking forward to it, too," Donovan dryly replied. He had enrolled at Madison after Hurricane Katrina forced his family out of New Orleans. He'd told me he was a star basketball player at a high school in New Orleans.

"Is Donovan the only one you see?" Camille blurted out.

Tori swung her head around, looked at Camille, turned up her nose, and said, "The only one that matters." Her girls giggled as she turned her attention back to Donovan.

"What?" Camille said. I was wondering what was wrong with me. Normally, I would've been the one to check someone like Tori, but Donovan had me all messed up in the head. Dang, I wasn't even being myself.

Tori ignored Camille as she adjusted her backpack. "Look, the homecoming dance is in two weeks and since you're new and all," she said as she licked her lips, "I was just wondering if you'd like for me to be your date."

Okay, I felt the old me coming back because I was about to straight stomp this skank. She sees him up here talking to me and she just gon' totally disrespect me. My knots were gone just that fast as I stepped toward her.

"Excuse me . . ."

She looked at me with disgust. I had to take a deep breath to keep from going off on her. Donovan, however, didn't give me a chance. He stepped in front of me.

"Tori, I'd love to go to the dance with you . . ."

I felt my heart drop. Camille and Angel looked shocked as well. Tori got a big grin.

"But," he continued, "I already have a date. I'm taking my girlfriend."

Tori's smile faded. I wanted to cry myself. How this fool gon' be all up in my face and he got a girlfriend? Low-down dirty dog.

"Oh," Tori said, obviously caught off guard. "I didn't know you had a girlfriend."

I wanted to tell Tori she wasn't the only one.

Donovan looked at me and smiled. "She didn't know it, either."

I looked confused.

"You have got to be kidding me," Tori said, looking back and forth between me and Donovan. "Jasmine is your girlfriend?"

"My girl"—Donovan turned away from Tori, stepped closer to me, leaned over, kissed me softly on the cheek, then pulled away—"Jasmine"—he kissed me again, then pulled away—"is the only person I want to go to the dance with."

"Oh. My. God," Angel said.

My sentiments exactly.

"This brother got major game," I heard Camille try to whisper to Angel.

Donovan put his arm around my shoulder and turned back to Tori, who was standing there with her mouth hanging open. "So, thanks, Tori, but no thanks."

Tori huffed, rolled her eyes, then stormed off with her girls following quickly behind her.

"You are the freaking man," Camille said as she shook her head in amazement. "That has to be the tightest thing I've ever seen in my life!"

Angel was still staring at Donovan all dreamy eyed. "Yeah, Jasmine. He's a keeper."

Donovan laughed. "I hope I didn't put you on the spot," he said to me.

I shook my head. With two kisses he had reverted me back to a driveling schoolgirl.

"It's just that girls like Tori make me sick," he said.

"So did you mean it about her being your girlfriend or was that all an act?" Camille said, getting all up between us.

I was so glad she said that because I sure was thinking it.

"Yeah."

"Yeah, what?" Camille said. "Yeah it was an act, or yeah you meant it?"

Donovan didn't take his eyes off me. "Yeah. I meant it. That's if she's interested."

"Shoot yeah, she's interested," Camille said, pushing my shoulder.

"I need to hear it from her," Donovan said.

I took a deep breath. I'd never had a boyfriend. Never

thought I'd have a boyfriend. I couldn't believe that the first one I got would be somebody like Donovan.

I smiled, trying to play it cool. "Yeah, I'm interested," I repeated.

Donovan laughed as he put his arms around me and pulled me into a big hug.

I no longer thought I'd died and gone to heaven. I knew I had.

9

Thank God they hadn't started yet. I was more than certain I'd be late to the meeting, but when I got there it looked like Alexis, Trina, Camille, and Angel were just getting there, too.

I brushed down my top and made sure my jeans weren't revealing any panty. All of a sudden, I wished I had some cute low-riders like Camille and Alexis wore and not these old baggy jeans I had on. Usually, I couldn't care less about my clothes, but I swear ever since I started going with Donovan last week, all I could think about was how I dressed. I guess because Tori always dressed so cute.

"What's up, Jasmine?" Camille spotted me first.

"Nothing much," I responded. I looked at Trina, who had just sat down at the table next to Alexis.

"We were just talking about what happened at the mall yesterday." Trina winked.

Since Donovan and I started going together I hadn't been around much. I missed the last two meetings because I had to babysit while Nikki and Jaquan went to some school function. So I didn't know what was going on with their little business.

"What happened?" I asked, easing down into an empty chair. I wondered where Miss Rachel was, 'cause honestly, I didn't feel like getting all caught up in their little boosting scheme.

"We'll have to fill you in later," Trina said. She turned to Alexis. "I found the perfect platform sandals to go with that throwback skirt I got."

I know lately I'd been concerned with my clothes, mostly because they were shabby. But that was really *all* they talked about—the latest clothes, this bag, those shoes. Give me a pair of jeans or a velour sweat suit and I'm usually straight. But I did have to admit, ever since I met Donovan, I have been thinking a lot about my appearance.

"What are you over there daydreaming about with that geeky smile plastered on your face?" Trina said, nudging Angel. They started laughing at me.

"I think *who* is more the question," Camille tossed in.

"Yeah, I heard you got the finest boyfriend in school," Alexis said.

"You heard right," I said. "But I'm stressing because he wants to go out and, well, you know how my mom is. She said I can't date until I turn sixteen."

"But you turn sixteen in three weeks," Angel said.

"I know, but she agreed yesterday to let me go to the homecoming dance. I don't want to push my luck by asking her can I go to the movies, too."

Camille nodded like she had it all figured out. "You'll just have to tell her you're going to the movies with us."

I smiled. "Yeah, that's what I'm going to have to do."

Just then Rachel came strolling into the room.

"So, are you ready to talk about the fall project?" she asked, looking at us.

Everyone nodded. At first, none of us were too keen on doing a youth project involving the Ten Commandments, I mean, how boring was that? But Alexis had come up with the idea for us to do a skit or something creative involving each commandment and it had actually turned into a lot of fun.

I reached for my backpack and couldn't help but notice that everyone else, Angel included, had designer bags. I shook off my thoughts and pulled out a piece of paper. "Well, I jotted down a couple of ideas about things we could do for the commandments where we don't have anything yet," I said.

Everybody looked at me like I was speaking French in Turkey or something. Rachel had told us all to bring some ideas to today's meeting. It wasn't my fault they didn't do it.

"Yeah, Miss Rachel, we all worked on the ideas and had Jasmine put them on paper," Camille joked.

Rachel looked at us like she knew Camille was lying. She shook her head. "Jasmine, since you're the only one who brought ideas, let's hear them."

I flashed a gloating look as I began sharing my ideas. I could tell Rachel was feeling them because she was getting all excited.

"Those are some great ideas. I think the kids—" Rachel stopped talking when the church secretary stuck her head in the door.

"Sister Rachel, there's a problem in the sanctuary that needs your immediate attention," the woman said.

Rachel nodded and turned toward us. "Girls, I'll be right back."

Rachel wasn't out of the door good before Trina turned toward us. "My cousin got a new shipment in."

Why was she talking like her cousin was some legitimate retail buyer? What she probably meant was "my cousin hit up another delivery truck." I'd overheard her telling Alexis that was how they got all the clothes. Her cousin would get the stuff off the trucks before it was even delivered to the stores.

"So when are we gonna open up shop?" Trina asked.

"Well, my mom is going out of town this Friday, so we can do something after school. If we start spreading the word, we should have a nice little flow," Alexis said.

I was trippin' at the ease over which Alexis seemed to be down with this. Even though she could be self-centered some times, she was still one of the sweetest people I'd ever met until Trina joined the group. Now she'd turned into someone I didn't even really know anymore.

"Okay, I'll let Sarah know. And you know once she knows everybody else will, too," Trina said.

Now, I was no Miss Goody Two-shoes or anything like that, but I just couldn't get into this stealing thing. I especially didn't understand why they needed to do it. And if you *were* goin' to do dirt, it seemed like to me you wouldn't let everybody and their mama know about it.

"Afterward, we can just hang out at my place and watch movies or something," Alexis continued.

Angel and Camille looked excited.

Trina looked at me. "So, are you in or what?"

"I guess," I said. I wasn't down with their little game but

I loved hanging out at Alexis's place. I mean, it *was* a mansion—why should I turn down a chance to live large? Even if it wasn't my place.

I scooted over toward the rest of the girls. "But we'll need Sonja to play like she's your mom, 'cause you know ain't no way in the world my mother or grandmother would let me stay if she thought we were gonna be there alone."

"Girl, don't trip. You know Sonja knows the deal." Alexis winked. "She's more than just the housekeeper."

"I think I can get my sister to babysit," Angel said. "So count me in, too."

It was settled. We'd hook up after school and meet at Alexis's house. Now all I had to do was make sure my grandmother would be on board. She could act funny sometimes. But I'd just have to make sure the house was clean, and maybe even fix something for dinner.

"I'll be there," I said.

"Unless, of course, Donovan calls and wants to do something instead," Camille joked.

I balled up a piece of paper and threw it at her. "Shut up, girl. Why you trippin'?" I laughed.

She ducked out of the way of the paper ball. "Please. I ain't mad at ya. Because if I had a man as fine as yours, I'd kick you busters to the curb as well."

We all laughed as we waited for Rachel to come back and wrap up the meeting.

10

I looked down the street for the twentieth time. Where were they? I mean, this was crazy. I'd been waiting almost an hour. Alexis called me, claiming they left the mall an hour and a half ago.

I didn't even want to think about what they were up to. I was just anxious to get away from my apartment. As usual, my brothers were getting on my nerves and I had to get out before my grandmother found something else for me to do.

I was just about to go back inside and call Alexis again when I saw them pulling up.

"Hey, miss, whatchu selling?" Alexis joked as they pulled up.

I rolled my eyes. "Dang! What took y'all so long? What were you doing in the mall, or do I even have to ask?" I shook my head as I climbed into the backseat next to Camille. She was talking away on the phone to someone and Trina was in the front seat jamming to the music.

Once we got to Alexis's house, I jumped out of the car and was walking up to the massive doors to Alexis's home when Trina summoned me back.

"Hey, you think you wanna give us a hand here?" she said.

When I turned and saw the trunk full of bags, my mouth dropped open.

"Where did you guys get all this stuff from? Dang! Y'all got the whole mall up in here!"

I could hardly believe it. There were shoes, designer baby clothes, purses . . . and everything still had regular tags and security sensors attached to them.

"How y'all gonna get these sensors off?" I asked, fingering a cute yellow blouse that had caught my eye.

"Don't worry about all that, you just help us get this stuff in the house before someone sees us," Trina snapped. I let her slide this time, but homegirl had one more time to snap at me.

It took us each two trips to the car to unload everything.

I looked at all the loot and just couldn't fathom how they were able to get away with doing this. Never in a thousand years would I have thought they, of all people, would stoop to stealing.

They spent the next two hours arranging the stuff in Alexis's room. I just sat off to the side and watched. I honestly didn't want to have anything to do with their little scheme. It was bad enough they had Camille and Angel all caught up in it.

By the time they were done sorting, it was like the room had been transformed into a specialty boutique. Alexis had ordered pizza but before we could finish eating, the doorbell rang.

"Is Sonja gonna get that?" Trina asked Alexis.

She shook her head. "I don't think so. Last time I saw her she was in the theater room cuddling a bucket of ice cream. I think she had a fight with her man, so she's drowning her sorrows, I guess."

I took it upon myself to go answer the door. Of course, the visitors were three girls, looking for clothes to buy. I led them to Alexis's room.

"Hey, Trina. What you got this time?"

"Hey, Crystal," Trina responded. "See for yourself."

Crystal and her friends looked toward the back of the room. Their eyes got wide and they started giggling.

"You guys are off the chain!" Crystal said.

"And Erica, girl, those Donna Karen warm-ups you wanted are here, too. You needed a size eight, right?" Before Erica could get all the way in the room Trina had the warm-ups separated from the other items for her.

The girls went through the mountain of clothes, shoes, and accessories. It was like they were in an all-you-can-eat candy store. They held up items in front of themselves in Alexis's full-length mirror, or ran over to her dresser holding up earrings and bangles. And Trina was acting like she was their personal shopper. The minute they put something down, she had something else for them to look at.

The doorbell rang again. "I'll be back," Alexis said as she took off.

"You think this looks good with my skin color?" Crystal asked me.

I smiled and quickly nodded.

"Yeah, and it would go good with those jeans over there," Trina said as she ran to pick up a pair of jeans.

When Alexis came back to the room, she had two more girls with her, who introduced themselves as Sara and Kym.

Just like Crystal and the others, Sara looked around the room and her eyes lit up. "Man, this is tight," she exclaimed. "It looks like you've got everything in here."

"I think we got those Apple Bottoms jeans you wanted. We also got the matching jacket to it. I know you didn't ask for that, but it is too cute," Trina said.

"Cool, lemme see them," Sara said.

The first group of girls spent close to eight hundred dollars. Sara and Kym spent another two hundred and fifty and Alexis and Trina were on their fifth set of customers. I could not believe that even after hours of showing off the stuff, the room still looked full.

Once Alexis ushered the last group of girls out of the house, she came running back to the bedroom.

"Okay, you guys think we should shut down the shop for tonight?" she asked.

"Did Cicely and her girls come through yet?" Trina asked. "I know they would call if they weren't coming. We should wait, then stop after they get here."

"Okay, deal," Alexis said. Twenty minutes later the doorbell rang again. I was hoping it was Cicely and her friends, because I was tired . . . and I refused to get caught up in their scheme. I knew it was wrong to be in there at all with all the stolen stuff and even help some of the customers with their selections, but I figured it was no harm since I hadn't stolen anything.

Cicely and her friends spent more than one thousand dollars. There were four of them, and they bought just about everything they tried on or put their hands on. How people had money to throw away like that was beyond me.

When Alexis showed them out and came back into the room, she sighed as if she had actually been working a real job.

"Okay, Trina, how'd we make out?" she asked.

"Five thousand eight hundred and ninety-three big smackeroos!" Trina sang.

My eyes nearly popped from their sockets. "Like five thousand as in five grand?" I couldn't believe it. "Are you kidding me?"

They all looked at me like I was crazy. But the truth was I had never seen that much money in my entire life. I couldn't believe they had actually made that much off that stolen stuff—and there was still a lot of stuff in the room.

"This is the real deal, Holyfield," Trina said. "I have to give my cousin twenty-five hundred, but the rest is all ours. Not bad for a couple of hours' work, huh?"

"Not bad at all," Camille said, shaking her head. I couldn't believe she, too, was getting caught up in this madness. Well, easy money would do that to you.

"So, are y'all ready to party, or what?" Trina said.

"Yeah. Levi from the basketball team said his parents are out of town so he's having a party at his house tonight," Camille said.

"Then it's on and poppin'. Let's get dressed," Trina said. I looked at her, wondering how she'd become the leader of our little group. If there was anybody that didn't need to be a leader, it was her.

I turned my head and caught a glimpse of myself in the mirror. "Oh, no. I'm not going to a party looking like this.

Especially a basketball party," I said. My hair was pulled back in my signature ponytail and I had on my usual warm-ups.

"Look, you can find something to wear out of all of this stuff," Trina said, pointing to all the clothes. "And I'll curl your hair." She dashed into the bathroom. I wanted to protest, but honestly, hanging around them was giving me a complex and I wanted something to really make Donovan proud to be seen with me.

What harm would there be in wearing something just for tonight and then giving it back as soon as we got home from the party? I had to wrestle with my conscience for a minute.

"You know what? That's all right," I finally said.

"Come on, Jasmine," Camille protested.

"Camille, I just wouldn't feel comfortable in this . . . in this stuff," I said, pointing to all the clothes.

"It's just for a couple of hours. It's not like you're keeping it," Trina said.

When I looked down at the outfits Trina was holding up, I felt myself growing weak. *Just a couple of hours, that's all.* I grabbed the outfits and made my way into the bathroom.

I quickly took off my clothes and pulled the top over my head. I was careful not to get anything on the clothes. I wasn't going to keep it so I didn't want to get it dirty. I pulled the material down over my shoulders, and tied the straps around my neck. It had a brooch right at the center of my chest, and the soft, flowing material flared out under my chest into a pleated skirt. I slipped on the jeans, which were studded with dazzling rhinestones. I looked at myself in the mirror and felt more special than I could ever remember. I stepped into a pair of wedge sandals and was ready.

"C'mon, now. Don't hog the bathroom. The rest of us still gotta get ready, you know!" Alexis yelled.

"Okay, here I come." I closed my eyes and giggled. Donovan was going to go ballistic. I opened my eyes to make sure this was really happening.

When I stepped out of the bathroom, my friends were speechless.

"Ohmigoodness!" Alexis said.

"Turn around," Angel encouraged.

"Dang, girl, you look hot. I like the way you mixed the two outfits. That's tight," Camille said.

I looked at my body. "What do you mean, mixed them?" I held out my arms, frowning.

"That's a minidress you're wearing with the jeans, but that works. It really does," Alexis said.

I ran toward the mirror and couldn't help but laugh at myself right along with my friends.

"You mean this is a dress? I thought it was a top," I said.

"Well, it's one of those you can wear as a mini, a skirt, or a top, like you obviously figured out. Girl, you're smokin'. Now let the rest of us try to pull ourselves together," Alexis said, rushing toward the bathroom before anyone else could beat her to it.

11

Cars were parked all up and down Levi's street. Alexis lucked out and pulled into a spot right in front of the house just as another car was pulling off. We all piled out and walked straight up to the front door. I was worried about the humidity making my curls fall, but when I ran my fingers through them, they still seemed tight.

We made our way inside. There were people everywhere and tables and chairs were lined up against the wall of the living room, but most of those seats were empty. The house was laid, with marble floors and chandeliers. I looked around in amazement. Did everybody have money but me?

Music was pumping loud and hard, so much so that it felt like the floor was vibrating. I glanced at the deejay, who was set up in a corner, bobbing his head to the beats.

Camille and Trina headed straight to the middle of the living room, which had been transformed into a dance floor. I looked around for Donovan.

"You want anything to drink?" Alexis asked.

I looked over at two guys pouring a clear liquid into the bowl of punch. I shook my head. "Naw, I'm straight," I said. The last thing I wanted was to be laid out somewhere drunk. That was definitely not the impression I was trying to give Donovan.

Alexis must've decided against getting something to drink as well, because she just stood next to me and Angel, swaying to the music. I was starting to relax and get my groove on when two guys showed up in front of us.

"Y'all wanna dance?" the shortest one said. I wasn't sure which one of us he was talking to. But Angel and Alexis jumped up and followed them out to the dance floor, snapping their fingers and moving to the music.

A thought flashed through my mind. I wondered what my grandmother would say if she knew that we were out partying when we were supposed to be at a sleepover. I shook it off and told myself I'd have fun while I could. There was no use in ruining the evening thinking crazy thoughts about getting caught.

I spotted C.J., the guy I used to have a crush on, heading my way. I was surprised that I wasn't the least bit fazed by the sight of him.

"What's up, Jasmine," C.J. said, as he flashed a grin I used to think was cute. Now it just looked plain stupid.

"What do you want, C.J.?"

"Don't be like that, girl," he said as he stepped closer to me.

I put my hand up to stop him from coming any closer. "You the one who made it like that. Don't think I forgot what a jerk you were."

"Boo, I'm sorry about that. I was young and stupid back then. I didn't know how to show you I was feeling you. But I'm older and wiser now," he said, stroking his chin.

"Boy, that was three months ago. You ain't that much wiser."

"Three months, a lifetime. What's the difference?"

I rolled my eyes and turned my head. That was when I spotted Donovan rolling into the party. I was about to push C.J. aside and go talk to him when I saw Tori slink up and drape her arm around his neck. He tried to move her out of the way, but she giggled and dragged him toward the dance floor. Even though Donovan was resisting and acting like he really didn't want to be bothered, his boys were whooping and hollerin', high-fiving each other. I felt my stomach turn as I heard one of them yell out, "Man, that chick is fine! You need to hit that!"

Donovan was obviously uncomfortable on the dance floor, but Tori didn't notice—or didn't care—as she gyrated, bounced up and down, and slithered all over him as T.I. rapped in the background.

I looked at C.J. and, without thinking, grabbed his arm and led him to the dance floor. I eased over toward Donovan. Tori saw me first and began putting on even more of a performance, trying to move in and kiss Donovan. I fought back a smile as he pushed her back.

C.J. started dancing. He looked like a fool with his no rhythm self. I couldn't take my eyes off of Tori, though. She looked like a pure freak the way she was grinding up against Donovan.

When the song ended and Usher's "Confessions" started playing, a huge smile crossed her face. She moved in and tried to put her arms around Donovan's neck and get him to slow dance with her.

At the same time C.J. was trying to pull me toward him.

I looked at him like he was crazy. I was a good foot and a half taller than him. I was not about to be hugged up with him on the dance floor.

Donovan looked up and caught my eye just as C.J. pulled my arm, begging me to slow dance. Tori saw him look at me and the smile immediately left her face. He said something to her, then pushed her off of him and walked my way. Her mouth fell open and she looked extremely embarrassed. I wished I had a camera because the look on her face was priceless.

"Hey, I didn't know you were here," Donovan said as he approached me. He looked at C.J. "What's up?"

"What's up with you?" C.J. asked, sticking his chest up like he was trying to flex. "We kinda busy right now."

Donovan, who was also several feet taller than C.J., laughed. "You gon' have to find someone else to dance with, patna. My girl doesn't slow dance with anyone but me." I ignored the shocked look on C.J.'s face as Donovan pulled me toward him. He took me in his arms and we swayed to the music. I felt weak in the knees.

"Hey, baby, how long you been here?" he whispered in my ear.

"Long enough to see Tori all over you," I said, trying to hide my jealousy. "She all but took off her panties and threw them at you."

Donovan rubbed my hair. "She can throw all she wants. I ain't trying to catch nothing she got. It's only one girl I want to be with, and that's you." He leaned back and looked me in the eyes. This time, I didn't look away. I stared right back at him. It felt like we were the only two people on the dance floor. We didn't say anything for a few minutes as we slowly rocked from side to side. Then he leaned in and gave me the deepest, most passionate kiss I'd ever had in my life. It was a kiss that felt like it went inside my body and touched my soul. I caught myself. That sounded like something corny Camille would say. But at that very moment, I knew where she was coming from when she talked about how much you can love a person. Because there was no longer any doubt. I was absolutely, positively in love.

12

The next morning the strong aroma of frying bacon and sausages woke me from my deep sleep. I opened my eyes and saw Alexis and Trina, who were in Alexis's bed, roll over. Camille was still sound asleep next to me on the air mattress. I pushed her arm away, which was elbowing me in the side.

"Ummm." Camille turned over and stretched. "Girl, I could live like this every day," she said, lifting her head from the pillow.

We woke up Angel, who was on the small sofa in the corner of Alexis's room. We slowly made our way downstairs into the kitchen where Sonja was stacking pancakes onto a plate that was already filled with waffles.

"Man, Sonja, look at all this food," Trina said.

"C'mon, girls. You better eat up. We don't want this food to go to waste," Sonja said.

There were pancakes, waffles, eggs, bacon, sausage, and hash browns. Sonja pulled apple, orange, and cranberry juice containers from the refrigerator.

I had never witnessed this much food on any given day. And for once I didn't have to worry about fighting my brothers for any of it. That was one of the things I hated so much about my life. We had so little that we were always fighting over scraps. If you didn't fight, you might be left out. Everything at home was just depressing. I couldn't remember the last time I just had fun with my family. It was nothing like when I was with Alexis and the other girls. I laughed, joked, and just had a good time. Even Trina was starting to be all right.

Before we could finish our breakfast, we heard noises at the front door and Alexis's dad walked in.

"Hey there. You girls having a good weekend, huh?" He smiled at everyone at the table.

"Daddy." Alexis leaned up to accept his kiss. "I thought you were coming home Sunday night," she said.

"I was, but my business wrapped up early, so I figured I'd come see what the Lansing girls were up to."

"Mom's not here. She went out of town," Alexis mumbled. "I thought she told you she was going."

"So, what are you ladies up to for the rest of this glorious Saturday afternoon?" He ignored her comment, then lifted a piece of bacon from Alexis's plate.

"We don't have any concrete plans. Why, did you need help with something?" Alexis asked.

"Thanks for being considerate, but I don't plan to do anything but hit the golf course as quickly as possible."

"Daddy, I'll be up to see you when I finish eating." Alexis smiled.

"Okay, pumpkin. Um, ah, I mean, Alexis." Mr. Lansing winked at his daughter before he left the kitchen.

I saw Trina watch Mr. Lansing as he walked down the hall. "Have I ever told you your daddy is just way too fine?

Too fine for his own good," she added, licking her lips. Alexis threw her napkin across the table at her.

"I'm gonna tell my mama on you," she teased. "That has to be the grossest thing I've ever heard."

"You know who's really fine?" Camille asked. When she had everyone's attention, she looked up from her plate and said, "That Donovan, that's who."

I couldn't hold back my smile.

Trina turned to me. "So, why don't you tell us what's up with you and him. Y'all clutched or what?"

"Ka-kling," Camille dramatically said.

I blushed as they all busted out laughing.

"So what are we gonna do today?" I asked, trying to change the subject. I didn't want to think about Donovan because I dang sure didn't want them to think he had my nose wide open.

"Well, whatever we do," Alexis said, getting up again, "we gotta be back here by three, four at the latest."

"Oh, customers, huh?" Camille asked. "You think they're gonna show?"

Alexis shrugged. "I don't know, but I told people we'd open up for business, so we gotta be here."

"You guys go ahead and finish eating. I'm about to go upstairs and take a shower," I said.

We ended up doing nothing but lounging around the house watching movies and nibbling on sweets. Just before three o'clock, the doorbell rang. Alexis walked over and opened the door. Some girl named Darlene and three others came bouncing into the room.

"Hey, girl. I'm so sorry we missed you yesterday. Thanks for opening up today, though," Darlene said.

The girls followed Alexis and Trina up the stairs and into the room. Me and Camille stayed downstairs in the family room watching TV. After about an hour and a half, they all walked out with bags of new outfits.

"Mo' money, mo' money, mo' money." Trina laughed as she waved a fistful of cash.

I shook my head. Trina was like a crack addict or something, only she was addicted to money. Me, I just didn't see their little enterprise lasting forever.

Trina stuffed the money into her purse. "On that note, I'm about to roll out. Got places to go, people to see, things to do."

"I'll bet you do." I laughed.

"Don't hate the playa. Hate the game," Trina said.

"I'm hating that ancient nineties' saying," I responded.

Our laughter was interrupted by the sound of a blaring horn outside. Camille looked out the window. "There's my mom. Angel, it looks like your mother is pulling up right behind her."

Alexis walked everybody to the door. We waved as Angel and Camille bounced down the driveway to their moms.

"You want me to give you a ride home, Jasmine?" Trina offered.

"Naw, girl. You go in the opposite direction." I looked at Alexis. "You still gon' take me home?"

"Yeah, no problem."

We said our good-byes and I went back in and plopped down on the sofa and picked up the remote.

"Let me go shower and change, then I'll drop you off," Alexis said.

I was flipping through the channels, not paying attention to anything because my mind had drifted back to Donovan. I looked up when I heard the front door open. Alexis's mom came into the living room looking like she had just stepped off a runway. She wore a silk tank top, white capris, and high-heeled sandals. She had a scarf tied around her head like she was a movie star or something. She seemed surprised to see me.

"Hello, there. You're Alexis's friend from the group, right?"

I stood up. "Yes, ma'am. I'm Jasmine. How are you?"

Mrs. Lansing sighed as she dropped her keys and her Chanel bag on the bar. "Don't even ask." She walked over and all but fell onto the sofa. "I'm just utterly exhausted."

I didn't know what to say. Her eyes were red, like she had been crying. She closed her eyes and took a deep breath. Her lip quivered like she was trying not to cry again.

"Are you okay, Mrs. Lansing?" I finally asked.

"I'm fine," she replied, sitting up. "Have a seat. What's your name again?"

"Jasmine."

"Have a seat, Jasmine. I would like to talk to you."

I looked around nervously. The last thing I wanted to be doing was sitting up having a conversation with Alexis's mom.

"You're good friends with my daughter, right?"

I nodded.

"Then maybe you can tell me why she hates me." She let loose the tears. "I just don't understand it. I try to be a good mother. Lexi doesn't want for anything. I give and I give and I give. And she just takes, takes, takes. And she still hates me."

Was she serious? Where was all this coming from? "Mrs. Lansing, I don't think Alexis hates you."

"Yes, she does. I see it in her eyes. Our relationship hasn't been the same . . . since . . . since . . ." Her voice trailed off.

"Since Sharon?"

Mrs. Lansing jerked her head around. "She told you about Sharon?"

"Yes, ma'am." Alexis had shared how they'd put her little sister in a home for autistic kids. Mrs. Lansing felt guilty about doing that.

Mrs. Lansing glared at me. "I guess you think I'm a horrible mother, too."

All I could think at that very moment was, why me? "I don't think anything, Mrs. Lansing."

"You don't understand. No one does. I put Sharon in that home because I didn't have a choice. I couldn't care for her. Now everybody hates me for it."

I stared at her. What did she expect me to say?

I breathed a sigh of relief when I saw Alexis coming down the stairs. She saw her mother's tear-streaked face and immediately turned up her nose. "Mother, what are you doing?"

Her mother dabbed her eyes. "I was just talking to Jasmine, that's all."

Alexis rolled her eyes. "We gotta go. Come on, Jasmine."

"See what I'm talking about?" Mrs. Lansing said as I stood up. "She hates me."

"Mother, please."

Her mother threw up her hands. "Fine, I won't bother your precious little friends." She stood, snatched her purse up, and stomped out of the living room and up the stairs.

Alexis grabbed her keys and headed to the door. "I'm sorry about that," she said. "I told you my mom had issues."

Normally, I would have protested. But this time, I had to agree with Alexis. Her mom had some serious issues.

13

I could hardly think straight. Donovan had called me last night and asked me to go to the movies. I was tired of making excuses and had agreed to go. But now that it was time for me to get ready, I was nervous as all get-out.

I had told my grandmother I had a Good Girlz community service event and wouldn't be home until sometime around midnight. I hated lying to her but I just couldn't risk them telling me I couldn't go.

When I emerged from my bedroom wearing a black prairie skirt and Nikki's lavender blouse, my brothers started giggling.

"She's wearing a frilly dress." Jalen laughed. Jaheim and Jaquan were right behind him. I did my best to ignore them because I wanted to make it out of the door without tumbling with my brothers. I knew I didn't need to be fighting minutes before I was going to meet Donovan. This was our first real date.

When we arrived at the theater—after he picked me up around the corner—I couldn't stop smiling. And the way he wouldn't take his eyes off of me didn't help matters any.

Donovan bought our tickets to *Idlewild* and we made

out way inside. As we stood in line for popcorn, someone ran up and smacked me on the butt. I turned around frowning until I saw Alexis and Camille giggling behind me.

"I told you that was her!" Camille said.

"In a skirt, nonetheless," Alexis commented.

"Um, you mind if we speak to you in private for just a sec?" Camille asked.

Donovan smiled as he moved up to the counter. "What kind of candy do you want before you go?" he asked.

"I'll take some Twizzlers," I said.

Once we were walking toward the ladies' room, Alexis said, "You really look good, girl."

"Thanks," I said.

"What y'all doing after the movies?" Camille asked.

I shrugged. "Going home. You know I can't stay out late and risk getting into any trouble."

They nodded as we all made our way into stalls.

After we handled our business, we walked back out in the foyer. "Well, since you all up in la-la land with your man, we gon' let you get back to him," Camille said.

"We're going to see *Final Destination Four,*" Alexis said.

"Ooooh, I wanted to see that," I said.

"You can dump Prince Charming and come watch it with us," Angel said.

"Yeah, okay," I replied. "Y'all enjoy the movie. I'm goin' back to my man." I smiled slyly as I walked back toward our theater.

I settled back in next to Donovan. As the movie started, he stretched his arm along my shoulders, hugging me. I scooted in close to watch the movie. Not that I was able to focus anyway. I could barely sit still. All I kept thinking about was what I would wear to the dance, how I'd get my hair done. There was just so much to think about. I knew Tori and her crew would try to show me up and I was determined she wouldn't make me look bad.

Before I knew it, the movie was over. Afterward, we went to IHOP, along with most of the students who had piled into the Edwards theater complex. I didn't want to stay out too late, because I didn't want to get in any trouble. I wanted to make sure I walked a straight line and stayed on top of school and housework so that my mother would buy me a new dress for the dance.

That night I got home nearly forty-five minutes earlier than I had promised. I thought for sure that would make me look good in my mom's eyes. My grandmother told my mother absolutely everything I did every day. I just hoped she'd report that, too. I stepped over my sleeping brothers who were stretched out on the living room floor and went into my bedroom.

I was surprised to see my grandmother up reading the Bible so late at night.

"Hey, Granny. What are you still doing up?" I asked.

My grandmother looked up from the Bible. "Chile, I don't sleep a wink until I know my babies are in safely. I pray that you guys make it in until the moment I hear you arrive."

I sat at the foot of my grandmother's full-sized bed, which sat on the opposite side of the room from my twin bed.

"So did you use to do this when Mama was a girl?"

"Use to? Hmm." My grandmother chuckled. "Your mother gets in at three in the morning. I usually fall off to sleep about three-fifteen. And when you're not here, well, let's just say I don't get the best sleep." She patted my hand. "But I am so happy to see you making friends. Even though I know you're at a friend's house for the weekend, I still talk to my God and ask Him to watch over you. Wherever you are."

Talk about feeling guilty. Here I was sneaking off to party and my grandmother was sitting up worrying about me. "Well, I'm about to shower and get some sleep. I love you," I said as I eased into the bathroom. "I'll keep it down, so you can go to sleep."

My grandmother smiled, then flicked out her nightlight.

I beat the sun up the next morning and was now in the kitchen whipping up eggs in a bowl as bacon sizzled on the griddle. I had some biscuits in the oven and grits boiling on the stove. After breakfast, I planned to clean the kitchen and start the laundry, so that my grandmother and mother would be able to relax.

Of course, everyone was excited to wake up to breakfast and they quickly gulped it down. Afterward, I cleaned up and quickly started to sort the clothes. When my grandmother tried to take over, I turned to her and said, "Granny, I wanted to give you a break for a change. So go kick up your feet and relax somewhere. I got this."

My grandmother laughed. "Chile, you ain't got to tell me twice. I need to catch up on Scripture for tomorrow's sermon anyhow."

"Now, Granny, you know and I know that there isn't a Scripture in the Good Book that you don't know by heart."

My grandmother swatted at me and giggled as she turned to leave.

"Everything looks so nice around here."

I didn't even notice my mother pop her head in the kitchen. When she gets in at three, she usually sleeps until about nine before she has to get ready to go to her other job.

"I made you a plate, Mama," I said as I removed her plate from the microwave.

"Thanks for breakfast, Jasmine," she said as she took the plate. "Oh, and I see you have some meat out. You fixing dinner, too?" she said, eyeing the fish sitting on the counter.

"Yes ma'am."

My mother leaned against the door frame. She looked over her shoulder then turned back toward me.

"I appreciate all that you do around here to help out with your brothers and to help your grandmother out. I just wanted to let you know." I was shocked because it wasn't often that my mom paid compliments.

"It's okay, Mom. I know you're swamped with two jobs. I don't mind at all."

"Well, I'm off today, so I'm taking your brothers to the park. Wanna come?"

"No, you guys go have a good time."

My mother ate while I finished cleaning up the kitchen. I spent the day cleaning up and cooking. By the time I finished stirring the beans to make sure they were soft enough, I was tired. I had fried catfish and prepared rice to go with the red beans. A few minutes before dinner I planned to make a green salad to top off the meal.

"Sure smells good in here," my mother said, walking into the kitchen. She sat down at the table and rubbed her feet. "Jalen wore me out today."

"Yeah, I learned from the best." I smiled. The house was spotless, the food was ready and I figured now was as good a time as any to ask my mom about a new dress for the dance.

"Ma, I was wondering. I wanna go to the homecoming dance next weekend. You think we could go shopping so I can get a new dress?" I wasn't ready to tell her I'd be going to the dance with a boy.

My mother's eyebrows inched upward. She closed her eyes and swallowed.

"I don't mind you going to the dance or even hanging out with your friends from that church group. But you know I just do not have the money to be going out and buying new dresses or outfits."

"But, Mama, this is important," I pleaded.

"So is eating."

"This isn't fair," I whined. "Just once I want to wear something new somewhere. I'm so sick of this."

"I suggest you watch your tone," my mother chastised. "Now, I agreed to let you go to that dance, but you just better go in that closet and find something to wear, or get something from Nikki. I'm sure she has something you can borrow."

I swallowed back tears. Nikki wore the tightest, shortest clothes she could find. I definitely wasn't trying to wear any of her hoochie outfits. Plus, I was too tall for her stuff anyway.

I didn't know what to say. I wanted to remind my

mother that I had kept my grades up despite the church group—except for the F in PE and the D in Algebra. But other than that, I'd been doing good.

"I know you're upset but it's just me. I'm taking care of everybody by myself. Maurice hasn't even paid his child support," she said, referring to my brothers' father and her ex-husband. Nikki's father had died shortly after she was born. I came along, then my mother got married and had my brothers.

"Maybe we should try to find my dad, Ma. You can get some money from him." The words escaped from my mouth before I even thought about it. I knew I had messed up as I watched my mother's eyes narrow. Her nostrils began to flare and I could hear her breathing. She stood up and moved closer to me. I backed up, until the sink prevented me from going any farther.

"Wwwh-at did you just say to me?"

"Um, ah, I don't . . . I didn't mean nothing by it, Ma," I tried to correct myself.

"Are you trying to say that I don't do enough to take care of you guys around here, because you can't get a new dress for a dance?" My mother glared at me in anger.

I shook my head slowly. "That's not what I was saying at all. I was just, um, I don't know, I thought—"

"You thought you would throw your father up in my face the minute you don't get what you want! I work myself to the bone to make sure you eat and have a safe place to sleep. I don't ask anybody for a thing, and you dare to tell me that I should try to find some deadbeat loser who could care less about you. I have the right mind to slap you into next week!"

I knew I was wrong for saying that to my mother, but the truth was, I had been feeling like that more and more lately. It wasn't just because I was jealous of Alexis's relationship with her father. I just wondered if maybe my life would be different if my father was around.

"Mama, I didn't mean anything by it," I stuttered.

"Oh, you meant everything by it," my mother hissed. "This is my last time telling you this. Your father does not exist. Stop asking me about him, stop with this fairy-tale dream that he's going to come back into your life. And if I ever hear you bring him up again I'm going to make you wish you hadn't."

My mother turned and stormed out of the kitchen as I buried my face in my hands and cried.

14

I hated to say it, but I was grateful when Rachel announced we had to wrap up the meeting early because she had a family emergency. I was still bummed out about my mother going off on me and being so totally against me trying to find my father. The girls noticed it.

"What's going on with you? You seem out of it," Camille said as we made our way out to the parking lot. I had agreed to ride to the mall with them. I didn't know why I did because that was only bumming me out even more.

"Yeah, I noticed it, too," Angel added. "Nothing's wrong with you and Donovan, is there? You guys make such a cute couple."

"Naw, it's nothing like that." I sighed. "Just trying to figure out what I'm wearing to the homecoming dance. My mom said she's not getting me a new dress and I cannot roll up in there looking all crazy. Especially with Tori trying to get her paws on my man."

"What to wear? That's all that's wrong? Then I'd say you don't have a problem." Trina flashed a wicked grin.

"What is that look for?" I asked.

"How about we work something out?" Trina responded.

I shot her a confused look. "What do you mean?"

"I mean, we can go to the mall right now, you pick out a dress you want, I make sure you get it, and all you gotta do is write a paper for me." Trina shrugged easily.

I shook my head. "I am not about to ask you to lift anything for me. What if you get caught? I wouldn't be able to sleep at night. I'll just have to find another way."

"Why are you trippin'? It's no big deal. Trust, I've been doing this so long, it's like second nature. I swear. But the choice is yours. Me, myself?" Trina pointed at her chest. "I'd be rollin' up in that dance looking like Beyoncé herself, only better!" She and Alexis slapped their palms together in the air and giggled.

I leaned up against Alexis's car. Stealing a dress was not the answer. I'd just have to think of something else. Maybe I could beg Alexis to loan me the money. Shoot, who was I kidding? Even if she did loan me the money, I didn't have a job so who knew when I'd be able to pay her back.

We made our way into Memorial City Mall and the Forever 21 store. We had just stepped foot in the door when I saw it. The dress to die for. It was a burnt orange color and the way it hugged the mannequin's body I knew I had to have it. I was surprised that I was even into a dress like that, but all I could think was how Donovan's mouth would drop open at the sight of me in that dress.

"Tori would be sick if she saw you in that," Trina stepped up to me and whispered. I couldn't help but shudder at the sudden image of my grandmother warning me that Trina was like the snake in the Garden of Eden. I shook off the image and turned my attention back to the dress.

Trina walked around and fingered the dress, pulling up the price tag. "Umph. One hundred forty-eight dollars. That's a lot of money." She looked toward the back. "But, what do you know, they have a rack of them right there in the back and they don't even have sensors." She smiled and dropped the tag. "Just five pages," Trina sang as she walked off.

I couldn't believe she was torturing me like that. I closed my eyes. *No, no, no,* I kept telling myself.

"Ohhh girl, that dress is off the chain!" Camille said as she walked up to me. "Go try it on."

Everything inside me was telling me to leave the dress alone and get the heck out of the store. There was no way I could ever afford it and trying it on would just be more torture.

"I can get a dressing room started for you," the clerk said. I actually jumped when she said that because I didn't see her sneak up behind me.

"Girl, go on," Camille said.

"Yeah, it won't hurt to at least try it on," Angel added.

What harm was there in at least seeing how it looked? I smiled, grabbed a size ten, and headed to the dressing room.

After I slipped the dress over my head, I pulled my ponytail holder off, shook out my hair, and stared at myself in the mirror. I looked like a celebrity or something. The dress hugged my body just right. It dipped in the front just enough to show a little skin, but nothing where I'd feel uncomfortable. I walked up to the full-length mirror and closed my eyes. I could see Donovan's reaction when he saw me in it. I could see Tori and her girls sick with envy. I could see me in this dress.

I took a deep breath, trying to come to my senses. No, I couldn't get caught up, no matter how badly I wanted this dress. I almost started crying as I pulled the dress over my head. Why couldn't I be rich?

I stepped out of the dressing room and almost ran into the clerk.

"How'd that work for y—"

I cut the saleslady off as I pushed the dress toward her and all but rushed out of the store. "I'll meet y'all at the food court," I told Camille as I raced past her. I couldn't believe how upset I was. But life was so unfair. Here I was, trying to do right, live right, and I couldn't even afford a stupid dress. I stomped toward the food court, trying to calm down.

Ten minutes later, I was sitting at a table in the food court sipping on a Sonic strawberry shake when my day went from bad to worse.

"Wonder how many calories are in a strawberry shake," Tori said as she and her friends surrounded my table.

Did she follow me around just to torture me?

"I bet it's a lot," one of her flunkies responded. "They're real fattening."

Tori laughed as I cut my eyes up at her.

"Hey, Donovan likes big girls, so I guess it's no big deal."

I pushed my chair back and stood up. She was about to be wearing my strawberry shake.

"Down, girl," Tori said.

"Look, tramp. I've had just about enough of you," I growled.

"Ooooh, I'm shaking in my shoes," Tori said. "I don't understand why you're all sensitive anyway. I wasn't trying to be mean. I just came over to show you what I was wearing to the homecoming dance." She turned to her girlfriend, who reached in a bag and pulled out a beautiful fuchsia halter dress. "It's a JLo design that will turn every head in the party. Including Donovan's."

I was straight about to slap this witch. "If your desperate behind thinks you can get Donovan, go for it."

"Oh, I intend to," Tori said as she stuffed the dress back into her shopping bag. "So, consider yourself warned."

"Ooooh, I'm shaking in my shoes," I said just as Alexis, Trina, Camille, and Angel walked up.

"What's going on, Jasmine?" Camille said.

I felt my nostrils flaring. "I'm two seconds from kicking Tori's a—"

"Such a violent girl," Tori said, cutting me off. "Come on, y'all," she told her girls. "Let's go before Jasmine has us up in here fighting like some ghetto trash."

I stepped toward her about to snatch that weave right out of her head. Camille grabbed my arm. "Chill, Jasmine. She ain't even worth it."

Tori laughed as they walked off.

"Ugggh," I said, slamming my chair against the table. "I can't stand that b—"

"What's all this about?" Alexis cut me off.

I took a deep breath. "Nothing. She just wants my man. That's all."

"Whatever," Angel said. "As if she stood a chance."

I thought about that bad JLo dress she pulled out and saw images of her sashaying past Donovan in that dress. And me, in one of Nikki's hand-me-down hoochie-mama party dresses. Why did people like Tori get all the breaks?

"I know you not gon' let her show you up at the homecoming dance, are you?" Trina said.

I sighed and stared at the floor. I looked up at everyone staring at me.

"Five pages?" I asked Trina.

She broke out a big smile. "Five pages on the Civil War. That's it."

"Okay. But only if you promise to do my hair and makeup, too."

"Girl, you ain't said nothing but a word," Trina answered, giving Alexis another high five.

I couldn't help but feel like I'd just made a deal with the devil.

15

"Go Jazzy. Get busy. Go Jazzy. Get busy, get busy . . ."

My girls had me hyped as they sang and waved their hands around me. I was surprising myself as I dropped it like it's hot on the dance floor with Donovan. Camille, Alexis, and Angel were all standing on the edge of the dance floor, probably shocked themselves because I was not one to get wild, but I was having the time of my life.

I couldn't remember a time when I had enjoyed myself so much at a school dance. When me and Donovan stood in line to take our homecoming pictures, everybody and their mama was complimenting me about my dress or asking where I had bought it.

Now, as Donovan held me close on the dance floor while we were jamming to R. Kelly's latest slow song, I was on cloud nine. Honestly, I wasn't the only one who looked good. My girls were holding their own, too.

This had to go down in history as the best school dance ever. When the song went off, I told Donovan I needed to go to the ladies' room. Alexis, Camille, and Angel caught up with me and we all went in together.

As we stood in the mirror touching up our makeup, I still couldn't believe this was my life. What a difference a year makes. When I met Alexis, Camille, and Angel, you couldn't have paid me to believe I'd be standing here in a dress, excited about a party. This was the way things were supposed to be.

"Excuse me."

I turned my head at the sound of the voice behind me.

"Um, I was just wondering, where did you get that dress?" the girl asked me.

"Oh. Forever 21." I smiled and turned back to the mirror.

"It's real nice. And you're one of only a few people who isn't dressed like somebody else. I've seen two people with my dress on, exact same color and everything," she said, sulking.

"Don't you hate when that happens," Alexis piped in.

"Thank you for the compliment," I told the girl as we made our way out of the restroom and back to the table.

"Why is it you girls can't go to the restroom alone," Phil, Alexis's date joked. "Do y'all help each other pee or something?" We rolled our eyes at him.

"Why do you have to be so disgusting?" Alexis said.

"You know your boy is nasty," I said. "Ouch!" I screamed in almost the same breath. I was about to ask Angel why she had kicked me. Then I noticed her motion toward a small crowd near the door.

I could feel the blood drain from my face. My mother, dressed in her security guard uniform, was looking all around the gym, calling my name. She spotted me, then came rushing toward our table.

"Ohmigod!" I said. Something had to be wrong. Why else would she come barging into the school dance? Without thinking, I jumped up from my chair to head off my mom. I heard Donovan calling after me, but I was determined to see what in the world was going on.

"Ma! What are you doing here?" I said as I nervously looked over my shoulder.

"Just who do you think you are talking to me like that?" my mother asked.

I closed my eyes and took a deep breath. "Ma, I didn't mean nothing by it. I'm just so shocked to see you here, that's all."

She rubbed her forehead. "I'm sorry to break up your fun, but we need to go. Your grandmother had to go see after Miss Mattie, who took a turn for the worse. Nikki's at work and Jaquan is still at basketball camp. The boys are having a sleepover. All of them are in the car and I got called in to work. So I need you to come home and watch them."

I frowned, looking at my mother like she was speaking Portuguese. I shook my head as if that might make this all go away.

"Wait a minute—you came to get me so I could leave the dance early to watch Jalen and his little stupid friends?"

"And? You act like that's a problem for you. I got called in to work the second shift tonight, so you need to come on. They needed me there five minutes ago," my mother snapped.

I was so mad, I didn't know what to do. I thought for sure I'd explode with anger. But I knew I just needed to go quietly before my mother embarrassed me anymore.

"Ma?"

My mother gave me a look that said, don't even try me right about now.

"Can I at least tell my friends that I need to leave and I'll catch up with them later?"

My mother looked toward the table where everyone was watching my every move.

"Go on. But make it quick. I need to get to work."

I pulled myself back to the table, despite all of the eyes gawking at me. People were pointing and whispering. I was so embarrassed, I just wanted to run from the building, go home, pack, and just disappear.

"Um, Donovan, I'm so sorry, but my grandmother is sick, I gotta go."

"What? Like right now? Do you want me to take you to the hospital?" he asked as he stood.

"No, no, you stay and enjoy yourself. I just um, I gotta be by her side."

"We can come with you," Alexis offered.

"No, girl. Y'all stay and hold things down. I mean, what are you gonna do in some stale, funky emergency room? Besides, I need you guys to keep an eye on my . . . well, you know I need somebody to look out for my interests," I tried to joke.

I could see the disappointment on Donovan's face, but I knew there was nothing I could do. When he walked over to me, I just knew he wasn't going to make this easy.

"At least I can walk you out, huh?"

"Maybe to the door. My mom is pretty upset," I lied.

"Oh, I can imagine," he offered as he put his arm around my waist. I felt horrible lying to him and my friends but I knew I had no other choice. I could never admit to them that my mother had pulled me away from a dance to babysit. I mean, this was too much.

By the time me and Donovan said our good-byes at the door, I had made up my mind about exactly what I had to do. And I'd start first thing tomorrow with my aunt, who despite her best efforts couldn't hold water if her life depended on it. If anyone knew how I could find my father, she did.

16

I knew I had to butter my aunt up. And if there was any way to do that, it was by telling her that her cooking was the best in the world.

"Auntie Teela, thank you so much for the food. It was delicious," I said as I watched my aunt move around the kitchen in her small townhome. She was the complete opposite of my mother—jolly all the time and hadn't worked in twenty years. She and my mom didn't really get along, but I tried to come visit her whenever I could. Especially since me and her daughter LaWanda were the same age.

"Thank you, baby. It's just a little something I threw together." She moved my plate to the sink. "You know your cousin is still at her dad's. She's gonna be so mad she missed you."

"Yeah, but it's like I told you on the phone last night, I really need to talk to you about something that, well, um . . ." I paused. "I just can't talk to my mom about this."

My aunt chuckled. "Oh, chile, you ain't gotta tell me how my sister can be. Remember, I grew up with her, so I know what she's like." She reached for my hands. "Now you know you can tell your Tee-Tee anything," she said. The phone rang and my aunt looked in its direction.

"Mmph, I need to get that. You don't mind, do you?" She dropped my hand before I could answer and dove for the phone.

"Hello?" Aunt Teela rolled her eyes dramatically and threw one hand to her hip. "Now I done already told you, you need to kick that bum to the curb. I don't see why you still chasing after his old tired tail," she said into the phone.

I sighed as I listened to my aunt. Here I was trying to find out some important information and she was on the phone gossiping. I shot her an impatient look.

"You know what, Evelyn? My niece is over here. She needs to talk to me about something she can't discuss with her mama." Aunt Teela tsked. "Hmm, tell me about it, chile. She betta not be pregnant, girl. My crazy sister would beat it right outta her and that's no lie." My aunt laughed.

I cleared my throat loudly and shot her another look.

"Anyway girl, lemme see what kind of teenage drama she got going on. I'll call you as soon as she leaves," Aunt Teela promised.

My aunt placed the phone back in its cradle and sat down across from me.

She folded her arms and leaned back in the chair.

"Okay, so you were saying you can't talk to your mom about this. Well, you made the right move by coming here. Now, who is he?"

I frowned at her. "Who is who?"

"Girl, you don't think I know what's going on here?"

"Aunt Teela, please. Can you hear me out?"

My aunt gave me a sideways glance and pursed her lips.

I started to wonder if it was a good idea to come to her in the first place. But I decided there was just no other way. I wanted to find my father as quickly as possible and I just knew my best shot was with my aunt.

"Well, I need your help," I said.

"Just call me the friendly family helper."

I looked down at the floor, then back up at my aunt. I just couldn't find the right words to say what I wanted.

"Look, Jasmine, you need to spit it out. Ain't nobody got all day. Whatever your problem is, you not the first and you ain't gonna be the last to deal with it. So come on here," Aunt Teela said.

"Okay." I nodded. "You're right, so here goes: I want to know if you could help me find my father."

Aunt Teela's head snapped back as if I'd slapped her. She looked confused.

"You want what? I mean, you ain't pregnant?"

"Pregnant? I'm not even . . . Never mind that, Auntie. I need you to tell me what you know about my father. I just want to talk to him. I can't talk to Mom about it, because, well, we both know how she feels about him."

"That's what this is all about? You're just looking for your father?" Aunt Teela threw her head back and started laughing. "I thought you had gone out there and gotten yourself knocked up." She hesitated a minute like she was debating whether she should say anything. She shrugged, then shook her head. "Your daddy lives right down the road in Galveston," Aunt Teela said easily. "I probably shouldn't be telling you this, but I been telling Jetola for years she needs to be honest with you. You ain't but about forty-five minutes from him."

My eyes got wide. "What do you mean, he lives in Galveston?"

"Galveston or La Marque, one of them," Aunt Teela said like she hadn't just dropped a bombshell on me.

I shook my head in disbelief. "Auntie, is it Galveston or La Marque?"

"It's one of them, just go to a school board meeting, you'll find him. Shoot, you can't miss him. You look just like him."

"I do?" I was having a hard time processing the idea that my father was less than an hour away.

"Yes, you do! I mean, *just* like him. No siree, Frank Sanders can't deny you."

I stared at her. I had so many questions. Had my father tried to deny me?

"Anyway, chile," Aunt Teela continued, "he's the superintendent of one of the school districts or some other important position like that down there."

"Did he know about me? Why didn't he ever try to get in touch with me? What's he like?" I rushed the questions out.

"Jasmine, what I done said already gon' start a holy war. You want more answers, you gon' have to get them from your mama. Or your daddy." She pushed back from the table and started putting dishes in the sink.

"Hmm, wait 'til I tell Evelyn you was just looking for your daddy. Girl, I thought you really needed help with something," she said.

"Auntie, you seem disappointed that that's all I wanted," I said. It was time for me to go. I had a lot to process.

"Shoot, I could've told you that over the phone, that's all I'm saying."

"Well, sorry to disappoint you by not having really bad news for you to help me with . . . but I really appreciate your help with this." I stood up as well.

"You know your mother is going to be hot with me, right?" Aunt Teela asked, not seeming the least bit worried.

"I know, and I'm sorry."

"Don't be sorry," Aunt Teela said. I swore I heard her laugh again as I made my way out the door.

I had caught the bus straight from Auntie Teela's to the meeting. I gathered Camille, Angel, and Alexis around so that I could fill them in on the details about my father.

"So if he's just right down the road in La Marque or Galveston, then we just go there and find him. It's not like he's far away," Camille said matter-of-factly.

I sighed. "Yeah, but what do you expect me to do? I can't just show up at the next school board meeting and say, 'I'd like to add an item to the agenda—Hey Mr. Superintendent, I'm your long-lost daughter. Where have you been all my life?' "

"I don't know about that, but what's the point in knowing exactly where he is if we're not going to do anything about it?" Alexis questioned. "Even though he works my nerves, I can't even think about life without my father. And if something prevented us from being together and I found out he was somewhere, girl, wild horses wouldn't keep me away."

I decided to say what was really on my mind. "I just can't believe he's been less than an hour away and he has never even tried to contact me. Maybe I should just leave well enough alone," I said, defeated.

Angel, who had been quiet most of the time, finally spoke. "I think you should go meet him, hear what he has to say. Then decide after that if you need to ever be bothered with him again."

"We'll go with you," Alexis said. She looked around at the other girls. "My cousin is a private investigator, so I'll have him do a little digging first, check to see if he's in Galveston or La Marque. Then we'll see if it's even possible for him to be your father."

"Your cousin could find all of that out?" I asked.

"Girl, please. My cousin is the best in the business. If there's dirt to be found, he'll find it. Then we'll see which night they have their school board meeting on. We'll make sure we're there early to catch him before he goes in. If not, we can stay late if we have to," she said.

I stared at my friends. They were serious as a heart attack. It was amazing how close we'd grown over the last year, especially because we were all so different. I couldn't help but smile.

"It's great knowing y'all got my back," I said.

"Always," Camille said.

"That's what friends are for," Alexis sang.

We all playfully groaned. "Please, do not break out into the Dionne Warwick song," Camille said.

"I'm mad that you even know who sings that song," I told Camille.

We laughed until Rachel came in and started the meeting.

17

The lunch bell had just rung, and people came racing out of the classrooms and into the halls as if someone was giving away free money. I stood by my locker wondering how no one was ever run over during these stampedes. Usually, I'd wait for my girls near Camille's locker, but I wanted to have lunch with Donovan today.

When he walked up and gave me a kiss on the cheek, I nearly melted right there in the hallway. It didn't hurt that Tori had walked by at that exact moment.

"I thought we could get pizza for lunch," he said as he took my hand and led me toward the cafeteria. I surveyed the packed and crowded cafeteria. Several cliques were in their normal spots.

Camille, Angel, and some other girls were off in the corner near the vending machines. And in the middle of all the chaos, Donovan took me by the arm and carefully guided me past the punkers, the skaters, and the cheerleaders, who sat staring at us. Even though it had been two months, people were still having a hard time understanding how the newest, cutest boy in school wanted me.

We walked over to a table near his teammates.

I sat down and Donovan went to get our Papa John's pizza from the vendor. The cheerleaders were still staring at us. I had no doubt Tori was dogging me out, but I knew she was just sick because she wanted Donovan. She wasn't used to rejection.

"I hope you like sausage. They ran out of pepperoni," Donovan said as he came back to the table. He put the box down in front of me. Before sliding next to me, he dug two sodas out of his pockets.

"By the way, our basketball banquet is coming up. I'm supposed to be getting an award. My coaches from New Orleans are coming up to present it to me. I was supposed to get it before the hurricane," he said.

"Oh, wow. What's it for?"

"It's for being a McDonald's All-American. It's supposed to be a really big deal." He took a sip of his soda. "But what would make it special was if you were there to share the award with me."

I blushed. Donovan always knew the right things to say and do. He was unlike any boy I'd ever met. I couldn't even believe I was getting all wrapped up in a boy. I was getting like Camille. But the funny part was, I wasn't even complaining.

I was a little worried that Donovan would pressure me for sex—I just didn't think I was ready to take it there. I heard all the time how the boys were always trying to get in your pants. Donovan asked me about having sex one time and when I told him I was a virgin, he seemed happy and hadn't really brought it up since. Come to think of it, he never did say whether he was a virgin or not. But as fine as he is, I doubt it very seriously.

"Do you get any money with that award?" I said as I realized he was waiting for an answer. "Can I share that, too?" I joked.

He leaned in and kissed me lightly on the lips. "You know it, baby. What's mine is yours."

"It must not be any money with it."

"Nope. Not a dime." He laughed.

We continued kidding around as we finished up our lunch. Just before the bell rang, Camille and Angel stopped by our table.

"Hey, Donovan," Angel said.

"Hey ladies," he greeted them.

"Jaz, are you riding home with us today?" Camille asked.

I looked at Donovan before answering. "It's okay with you, right? I mean, we can hook up later."

"Oh, yeah." He nodded, stuffing the last of his pizza into his mouth. "You know I got practice after school, so I'll call you later."

"So, meet at my locker?" Camille said.

"Alexis called. She got some information about that meeting in La Marque," Angel commented.

My eyes grew wide. "No way!"

"I told you we'd handle it," Camille said. "But we can talk about it later."

I was shocked. It had only been a couple of days. I never expected anything to come of that.

"My locker at three forty-five," Camille tossed over her shoulder, before she and Angel mixed into the crowd flowing toward the cafeteria doors.

I had a hard time making it through the day. I could hardly concentrate.

Alexis and Trina met us after school at the Starbucks in Meyerland Plaza. Camille and Angel wouldn't give me any info until we got to the coffee shop, saying all Alexis had told them was that we should meet at Starbucks.

Once we arrived at the coffee shop, we saw Trina and Alexis already sitting at a small table in the corner.

"Ewwww . . . What's wrong with you, Jasmine?" Alexis said as we approached the table. She must've been talking about the distressed look on my face. "I would think you'd be happy about getting information on your father."

"Nah, it's nothing like that," I admitted as I sat down.

"Well, what's wrong, then?" Trina said.

I sighed. "Well, it's just Donovan asked me to the basketball banquet, and of course I have nothing to wear."

Alexis laughed. "Who would have ever thought Jasmine Jones would be worried about what she's wearing?"

"On the real." Camille chuckled.

"You're joking about not having anything to wear, right?" Trina said. "I mean, you saw how easily we solved that problem for the homecoming dance."

"No, I'm not joking," I replied. "And the homecoming dance was a onetime thing."

"Girl, please, you know all you gotta do is go pick up something at the mall, and I do mean 'pick up,' " Trina joked.

I rolled my eyes. That was Trina's answer to everything. "Come on, y'all, I don't even want to get into that right now. Let's talk about what you found out," I said, turning my attention to Alexis.

The banquet was a whole three weeks away. I figured if nothing else, I'd find a way to buy a new dress before then.

I'd been saving a little money in a jar hidden in the back of my closet. I had about fifty dollars. Worst case scenario, I'd use that.

Alexis shifted in her seat. You could tell she was excited. "Okay, my cousin did some checking. It's a woman over the Galveston School District and an old, fat, Jewish man over the Texas City School District, which is right next to La Marque. I figure the woman is out and so is the old, fat, Jewish man, unless there's something you're not telling us, Jasmine."

"Yeah, right. I'm half Jewish." I swatted at her. "Quit playing and finish."

"Okay, it was pretty much the same story at all the districts in that area down there, except for the La Marque School District. Wanna guess what their superintendent's name is?"

I looked at her, stunned. "Frank?"

She nodded. "Dr. Frank Sanders. A tall, good-looking black man."

I leaned back in my seat at a loss for words. Could that actually be my father?

"Turns out, he is married," Alexis continued. "Has been for twenty years. Pretty straitlaced. Clean record, pillar of the community. Oh yeah, except for a little affair he had sixteen years ago."

"My mother?"

"I'm assuming so. My cousin said he wasn't able to find out who it was with since it was so long ago. Only that his wife filed for a divorce, saying he had been unfaithful. She ended up staying with him."

I shook my head in disbelief, trying to take everything in.

"Your cousin is off the chain," Trina said.

"Tell me about it. He has his own private investigation company and can find out just about anything," Alexis said.

"You think he can find out where Osama bin Laden is?" Trina asked.

Camille blew a breath. "Do they ever shut up on your planet?"

Trina shrugged and leaned back in her chair. "I could use the reward money, that's all I'm saying."

"Man, this is great news," Angel said to me.

"I think so," Alexis said. "I did some checking on my own and found out the La Marque School Board meets the first Tuesday of every month at seven. So, I figured we just need to show up about thirty minutes early and catch your dad before he walks into the building."

"Just like that, huh?" I asked.

"Just like that." Camille added, "Girl, I'm all excited about this. I can't believe your daddy's been right here in the same state, same city almost, and you had no idea."

"I know." I gazed out the window of the coffee shop. I couldn't believe it, either. But what I really couldn't believe was the fact that this man had a daughter less than an hour's drive away and he had no interest in her whatsoever.

"Did he know about me?" I asked without looking away from the window.

"I don't know," Alexis said. "That's all my cousin could find out. At least, that's all he would find out for free."

I didn't want to admit it to my friends, but I was most worried about what would happen if I went to see him and he refused to claim me. To have my own father reject me again would be devastating. And to have him do it in front of my friends . . . I just didn't know if I could handle that.

I closed my eyes. Maybe telling them about this hadn't been a good idea after all.

"So I guess the question is, are we going to La Marque or not?" Angel said.

This was all so overwhelming to me.

"Hey, guys, I really love you all for what y'all did. You know, with finding my dad and all, but I'm just not ready yet. I mean, how often do they have these school board meetings?" I asked.

"Once a month," Alexis said.

"Well, maybe by next month I'll be ready to go. Right now, I just can't. I hope you guys aren't mad at me." I offered up a weak smile.

Oh, I was going—I just wasn't going with them. Nope, to have my mother totally embarrass me was one thing, but to then have my father do it as well? That was a chance I didn't want to take. But I was definitely going. I couldn't wait until Tuesday.

18

I took a deep breath, closed my eyes, and said a silent prayer. When I was done, I exhaled and walked around the corner of the massive building. I didn't know what I would do if this didn't work. I hadn't planned that far in advance. I had lied to Aunt Teela and told her that I had my driver's license so she'd let me use her car to drive down here. That had been like pulling teeth. I think Aunt Teela gave me the car just so I would have to come straight to her house when I got back and I'd be able to fill her in. Luckily, I did know how to drive, thanks to driver's ed and a few spins around the block with Alexis as my coach.

It took me a minute to get down there because I was careful to drive the speed limit. I parked, then walked up to the door of the administration building and pulled it open. There was a receptionist sitting at the desk. She got a strange look across her face when she saw me walk up to her desk.

"Um, I'm here to see Mr. Sanders. He's the superintendent, right?" I was so nervous, I thought I was going to pass out.

The woman looked at me like she had seen a ghost.

"Dr. Sanders is here. But do you have an appointment? He's got a meeting he's preparing for," she said, looking nervously around.

I looked around the lobby. I saw a closed door straight ahead with his name on it. I thought about just running back there and telling him who I was. The woman must've read my mind.

"Why don't I tell him that you're here? What's your name?" She finally smiled.

"Um, my name?"

"Yes, dear, your name. You can't go in to see the superintendent if I don't know your name. How will I announce you?"

I fought back the tears that were threatening to come through. I was this close to finally meeting my father, something I'd dreamt about for years. "My name is Jasmine, um, Jasmine Jones," I mumbled.

Before we could finish our conversation, a voice rang out.

"Miss Brewisky, I need you to . . ." He stopped speaking. When I looked up, I thought I was staring into a mirror. Sure, he was an older man, but he was tall like me, had the same cheekbones, same eyes, same color skin, even the same sandy brown hair. He was frowning from confusion, but there was no denying we had to be related.

"What's going on here?" he asked, looking first at the receptionist, then at me.

"She's . . . she's here to see you," Miss Brewisky said, her eyes wide.

He looked at me like he was still trying to figure out why we looked so much alike. "May I help you?" he said.

"Um, I um, I needed to talk to you." I felt my voice cracking. His face finally seemed to soften a bit.

"What's this about?" he asked.

I looked at the receptionist, then at my father.

"I need to go." Miss Brewisky rose from her chair, shook her head, and grabbed a file. "I need to go deliver this. I'll be back in five minutes."

I looked at her as she scurried off toward the back.

"My name is Jasmine Jones, and um, I-I'm your daughter." No sense in trying to beat around the bush. Not that I could even if I wanted to. I was so nervous that as soon as I opened my mouth everything just came pouring out.

"I don't want anything," I continued. "I just wanted to know why you never came to see about me. I just wanted to meet you."

He looked around the lobby, obviously stunned. "Follow me, please," he said, motioning to his office.

"Who are you? And what are you saying?" he said as soon as we were in his office and he'd closed the door.

"Jetola Jones. In Houston. Do you remember her?" I didn't give him time to answer. "She's my mother. My aunt Teela said . . ." I wasn't able to finish my sentence. He took me into a big bear hug.

"Looking at you is like looking at an older version of Darla and Carla," he said, pulling himself away from me. He stared at me and smiled. A single tear fell down his cheek. "I had no idea. I can't believe this. I had heard rumors, b-but when I asked your mother about it . . . I-I had no clue." He was stuttering. He was just that shocked, I supposed.

I had to catch my breath. This was definitely not the reaction I had been expecting. Could he be telling the truth? Was he serious?

"You've got to believe me when I say I didn't know. Me

and your mama . . ." He paused and shook his head. "I was at a rough time in my life and your mother was there for me. But—I had no idea," he said, squeezing me again.

I was stunned. I was ready to go off on him, yell at him for abandoning me. "But she said you left us." This wasn't making any sense. Had my mother just outright lied?

"I couldn't leave what I didn't know I had." He rubbed my hair. He looked like he was still in shock. "I saw Jetola a few years back, and she never said a word. Never gave me any inkling that you existed. Just look at you. Any fool could tell you're mine," he said.

When Miss Brewisky came over his speakerphone and reminded him of the meeting that he needed to get to, he even told her to tell the assistant superintendent to fill in for him. For the next two hours, I sat and told my father all about my life. After that, we walked out to his Lexus and got inside. I felt like a princess, riding in that luxury car. Everything was moving so fast. I smiled as I envisioned my life now that my father was in it.

We ended up eating at a restaurant on the Kemah boardwalk. I was on cloud nine as we spent the rest of the evening talking and catching up. He seemed so excited to know that I existed. He had one son older than me, who was away at Howard University, and twin daughters, two years younger than me. He'd been the superintendent of the La Marque School District for the past two years.

As he shared details of his life with me, I couldn't help but wonder how *my* life would have been if I had been raised with him. And I definitely wondered where I'd fit into his life now that he did know about me.

After we finished up dinner, my father dropped me off back at the administration building.

"Are you going to be okay driving home?" he said. "I don't know what I was thinking, keeping you out this late. You shouldn't be on the road by yourself."

It felt so good having a father to worry over me. "It's okay. It's not even dark yet," I said.

He smiled. "Listen to me, sounding like an overprotective father."

I nodded. I liked the sound of that. I opened the car door to get in.

He grabbed my arm. "Jasmine, I'm glad you found me. I really am."

I flashed a smile. "I am, too."

"You call me when you make it home. You still have my cell phone number?"

I patted the pocket of my jeans. "Right here. I'll call you and let you know I made it."

"And you'll call me every day after that?"

I reached up and hugged him. "Of course." He kissed my cheek as I got in the car.

I looked in the rearview mirror and watched my father standing in the parking lot watching me drive off. I waved one last time and settled in for my forty-five-minute drive home.

This had to be one of the best days of my life. Next to any time I spent with Donovan, of course.

On the drive home, my mind went back to countless conversations with my mother, where she'd made my father out to be some kind of monster. My mom had done a lot of foul stuff as far as I was concerned. But this, I thought, this had to be the worst.

19

This was the second weekend in a row I'd spent with my father and the second time I'd felt my heart drop when it was time to leave. This time, at least, he was taking me home, so I was getting a little extra time with him.

When we pulled up in front of my apartment, I didn't want to get out. I didn't want him to leave because every time he did I was scared I would never see him again. He must've been reading my mind because he reached over and touched my hand.

"I don't plan on losing you again. I don't know why your mother didn't tell me, but you have to know that I would never abandon my responsibility." He smiled and shook his head. "Man, it's amazing how much you look like your grandmother, too. When I first saw you it was like looking at pictures of her."

I smiled, wishing I'd gotten a chance to meet her. My father told me she'd died last year. My mother had taken so much from me.

"Do you wanna come up and meet my other grandmother?" I said.

"Leona? She lives with you guys?"

I nodded, forgetting that he would know my grandmother. We spent so much time talking about his family, his job, my school, and my sister and brothers, that we never talked about my mother or grandmother. I had tried to steer the conversation there a few times, but he always changed the subject.

"You can come up and say hi," I said. I hadn't told anyone but the girls about finding my father. I was ready for my grandmother to know. I knew she'd tell my mother. I'd been too scared to bring it up.

My father hesitated, like he was debating what to do.

"Sure, it's long overdue," he finally said.

We walked up to the apartment door, and I took a deep breath. I searched for my keys and opened the door to an embarrassing sight. It was nothing out of the ordinary. My brothers and some of their friends had transformed the living room into a pigsty. Junk was everywhere and I wasn't even going to attempt to get their attention as their eyes followed colorful characters on the screen.

"You guys better start cleaning up that living room before I beat you into next week!" I heard my grandmother's voice barreling from the back room.

"Some things never change," my father said with a smile.

I looked at him. I wished I had never suggested he come up.

"I'm just remembering your grandmother's voice," he said. "She threatened me many a day with that voice."

When my grandmother appeared in the doorway, she dropped the glass she was holding, looked at my father, and shook her head.

The crashing noise made me jump, but for some strange reason, I felt incredibly safe knowing I was in my father's presence.

"Well, look what the cat done drug in," my grandmother said. She didn't crack a smile.

"Hello to you, too, Leona," he said.

Suddenly my grandmother's icy stare had me feeling uneasy. "Look what you done made me do," she said. "Girl, rush and get me the broom before one of these boys cuts themselves."

I wasn't sure why, but I didn't want to leave my father there alone.

"So what are you doing here?" I heard my grandmother ask him. I quickly grabbed the broom and dustpan and ran back to the living room. I didn't want to miss a single thing.

"Just building a relationship with my daughter," he said.

"Is you now?" my grandmother said. They almost seemed to be doing a stare down. But even though my grandmother was way shorter than my father, she didn't seem the least bit intimidated.

"Are you Jasmine's daddy?" Jalen said, tugging on my father's pants leg.

My father looked like he didn't want to take his eyes off my grandmother, but he shook off whatever it was that was unspoken between them. He looked at Jalen and smiled. "I am. And you must be Jalen." I was surprised he'd remembered my brother's name.

Jalen nodded, flashing his cute dimples. "That's me."

"Boy, get on back over there and watch them play that game," my grandmother said as she shooed him away.

I started cleaning up the mess. "Suffice it to say, I'm sure your mama don't know nothing about this," my grandmother said.

"Maybe you should call Mom at work," I said. I was thinking if my grandmother broke the news over the phone, it would give my mom time to calm down on the way home.

"Oh, I'ma call her, all right," my grandmother snarled as she frowned at my father. She spun around on her heels and walked back into the kitchen.

When she emerged a few minutes later, she held the phone out toward me. "Your mother wants to speak with you," she said.

My father's cell phone rang. He glanced at the caller ID, then stepped to the side and turned his back, speaking into the phone in a low voice.

I took the house phone and got ready to give my mother major attitude. I didn't get the chance.

"Have you lost your mind!" my mother screamed. "Why did you bring that man into my home? How did you find him? Why would you do that?"

I tried my best to remain calm. "You wouldn't give me any answers. So I searched for them on my own. And I'm glad I did. He didn't even know I existed. Mama, how could you do that?" I felt myself getting mad all over again. "He wants to know me. He wants a relationship with me and you took that from me . . ."

I couldn't help it anymore. The emotion seemed to overtake me and I felt my shoulders slump as I burst into tears.

My father walked over to me, took me in his arms, and

eased the phone out of my hand. I heard my mother screaming at him and he just kept saying, "Uh-huh."

"Jetola, we need to sit down and talk. Now is not the time, but believe me when I tell you, this is far from over," he said. He pushed the end button on the phone and pulled me closer as I continued to cry on his shoulder.

Normally, there was no way I'd have ever let my brothers see me bawling, but right about now, I didn't care. Right about now the only thing that mattered to me was how safe I felt in my father's arms. It was a feeling I'd been missing all my life. And I knew one thing—I didn't care how mad it made my mother or what she said—I wasn't going to let anyone take that away.

20

My vision was clouded by tears as I stared at my mother. But I was determined not to cry. I wanted so badly to say what was really on my mind but I just stood there biting my lip.

My mother stood in the entrance to my bedroom, her chest heaving up and down. Strands of her hair had come loose from the tight bun she always wore.

"I don't believe you," she hissed. "Not only do you go behind my back! Then you have the nerve to smart-mouth me?"

I hadn't meant to get smart with my mom but when she came home and started yelling at me for bringing my father here, I just kind of snapped and told her it wasn't my fault she messed with a married man who didn't want her. And she had no right to keep him from me. Oh, she went straight ballistic. If my grandmother hadn't been home, they'd be picking out flowers for my casket right about now.

"Jetola, calm down," my grandmother said.

"I just wanted to know my daddy." I sniffled as I wiped my nose.

"If you needed to know your daddy, you would've known your daddy," my mother growled. She turned to my grandmother and threw up her arms. "After all I've done for her. As hard as I work. She gon' do this. Then she's gon' try and stand in judgment of me!" My mother was crying, something I'd never seen before.

I peered from the side of the bed. I noticed Jaquan, Jaheim, and Nikki peeking in the door, no doubt trying to be nosy and see me get my butt beat.

"You don't know nothing about what I was doing!" My mother lunged at me again. I scurried out of the way again.

"I'm sorry, Mama. I didn't mean it."

"Oh, you meant it, all right. You meant every word." My mother was trying to catch her breath as tears fell down her face.

"Jetola, why don't you let me talk to Jasmine and you go sit on the balcony and calm down." My grandmother gently took my mother's arm.

My mother stared at me. It was a glare that seemed to go straight through my body. I know my eyes were filled with fear.

"Don't you ever disrespect me like that again," my mother said calmly as she caught her breath. "I gave you life. Don't you ever, as long as you walk this earth, disrespect me again."

"Jetola, go on," my grandmother said.

My mother gritted her teeth before turning and storming out of the room. Jaquan, Jaheim, and Nikki all took off, trying to get out of her way.

My grandmother stood with her arms folded across her chest. "Do you have a death wish, girl?"

I came from around the side of the bed. "Granny, I wasn't trying to hurt her. I just wanted to know who my daddy was."

"Some things are best left unknown." My grandmother shook her head. "And you sho' coulda handled this a whole lot better. Sit down," she said, pointing to the bed.

I sat next to my grandmother, catching a glimpse of myself in the mirror as I sat down. My hair was all over my head—I looked a hot mess.

"Now, you want to tell me what you were trying to prove by tracking down your daddy when your mother had made it clear that she didn't want you to do that? And then, on top of that, bringing him here?"

I plopped down on my bed. "Granny, she doesn't have the right to keep me from my father." I lowered my head and started playing with my fingers.

My grandmother sat on the bed next to me. "Sometimes we don't always understand our parents' decisions, but we have to trust they know what they're doing. Sometimes they do. Sometimes they don't. Just like God. We don't always understand why He does some of the things He does, but we have to trust that He has our best interest at heart."

"You're right, because I don't understand why she wouldn't want me to know him. He seems so perfect."

"Chile, ain't nobody perfect but God."

I let out a long breath. "Granny, how could Mama have messed with a married man? What type of woman was she?" My mother never had been one to date a bunch of different men. All she did most of the time was work. "I never would've expected her to do something like that," I said.

My grandmother squeezed my hand. "There's a lot you don't know about your mama. She's had a hard row to sow. So don't sit there and try to judge her, okay? Don't judge nobody. Leave that to the Lord."

"But I don't understand. He's been married over twenty years. And Granny, he was so happy to meet me. He said Mama had kept me from him all these years. How could she do that? Why *would* she do that?" I needed to make sense of all that had unfolded.

"Like I said, everything ain't meant for us to understand," my grandmother said as she pinched my cheek.

I looked at the door. Jaheim was peeking his nosy behind through the door again. I turned back toward my grandmother. I had planned to just ease into what I really wanted to say. But I was so upset I decided to just blurt it out. "Well, I want to go live with him. And he said I could come."

"Did he now?" My grandmother nodded like she wasn't the least bit surprised.

"Yes, and I want to go. Granny, no disrespect, but things would just be so much better. He's a doctor and he lives in a huge house in a gated community. It has five bedrooms." I was feeling better already about the prospect of my own room, living in a big house, with a normal family. It meant I'd have to transfer schools again, but I didn't care. I'd finish out the semester, then transfer to school down there.

"Better for who?"

I lowered my eyes, but didn't respond.

"Oh, I get it. Because he lives in that fancy house in that ritzy neighborhood, you think he's the be all to end all?" My grandmother laughed.

"That's not what I meant."

"Oh, you said what you meant." She stood. "Our little apartment is nothing compared to his mansion and you think that living there will make your life so much better?"

This conversation was not going the way I wanted it to. The last thing I wanted to do was hurt my grandmother's feelings as well. "I just want to go live with him, that's all."

"Let her go."

Both my grandmother and I turned our attention back to the doorway. Neither of us had noticed my mother come back in.

"Jetola, she's just upset—you both are. Neither one of you is thinking clearly," my grandmother said.

"Oh, I'm real clear. Let her go. Since I'm such a horrible mother and our life here is so miserable, let her go. Let her go live with her daddy and his wife. Then she'll see how bad I really am." My mother turned and stormed out of the room. I heard the front door slam a few minutes later. I felt the tears I had been fighting back earlier begin to fall down my face. But I didn't know if they were tears of sadness or joy.

21

I knew I probably should have shown some type of sadness right about now. After all, Nikki and my brothers were sitting in the living room looking all pitiful and stuff.

My grandmother was in the kitchen cooking, trying her best to look busy. Not surprisingly, my mother was nowhere to be found. She'd left without even saying goodbye. *If that's the way she's going to be, fine. I'll see her when I see her,* I thought.

I threw my last bag over my shoulder. My father was waiting down in the car. He'd come up, spoken to everyone, then carried some bags back out.

"I can't believe you're going to do this," Jaquan said. I thought he'd be glad to see me go, as much as we fought.

"Why she get to be the lucky one?" Nikki moaned.

I ignored their comments, instead leaning down toward my youngest brother. "Jalen, you be a good boy, okay?" I said.

"Don't leave, Jasmine. I gon' miss you," Jalen cried.

"It's, 'I'm going to,' " I corrected.

"I'm going to miss you," Jalen repeated.

"I'm only moving to La Marque. You remember when

we went to the beach in Galveston?" He nodded. "That wasn't that far was it?"

He shook his head as he sniffed.

"So, see, I won't be far away. And I'll come see you all the time. My dad's letting me use my half-brother's car. He's away at college."

"You get a car!" Nikki exclaimed. "Man, that sucks!" she said, as she turned and stormed out of the room.

I ignored her. "Jalen, don't be sad, okay. I promise I'll come back and see you."

"Unh-unh. 'Cuz Mama said if you leave, you wasn't coming back," Jalen said.

"Mama's just mad right now," I said as I stood up. At least I hoped she was. But truthfully, at that very moment I didn't really care. I just knew I was finally getting out of this godforsaken house and going to live the life I was born to live.

"And if she won't let me come back, maybe you can come see me and we can go to the beach and stuff."

"For real?" Jalen said.

I nodded as I reached down and hugged him. I looked at everyone. Jaquan and Jaheim walked over and hugged me. Jaquan pushed my head.

"Who am I gon' fight with now?" He tried to smile, but I could've sworn his voice cracked.

"You just gon' have to find somebody else to get beat up by," I joked.

"Beat up? You ain't never beat me up," he said.

"Please, boy," I said, pushing his shoulder.

His smile faded. "I'm gon' miss you, sis."

"I'm gonna miss you, too." I looked at everybody. "I'm

gonna miss all of you." I took a deep breath. "Let me get out of here." I walked toward the kitchen. My grandmother was at the stove, stirring something in the pot. "Granny, I'm gone."

"Umm-hmm," she replied. "You be safe."

I stood there a minute because she wouldn't turn around. "Well, I'll see you later." I turned to leave and had just reached the door when she stopped me.

"Jasmine, come here."

I walked back toward her with my head lowered. She lifted my chin. "I hope you know what you're doing, baby girl. Sometimes our blessings are disguised and what we don't think is a blessing, is. And what we think is a blessing, isn't."

I didn't quite understand what she was saying and chalked it up to just another one of her ramblings.

She pulled me close as she hugged me. "For your sake, I hope he's changed," she whispered.

"Who's changed?"

My grandmother released me from her embrace and squeezed my hand. "Don't you worry. I'm going to be praying for you, baby girl. God will keep a watchful eye over you. I hope you find the happiness you looking for."

I forced a smile at my grandmother and took one last look around the room before making my way outside.

As I walked down the stairs toward my father's car, my forced smile turned into a real one. And as sad as I probably should have been about leaving my family, I couldn't help but feel this was the happiest day of my life.

22

I was so nervous, I thought my heart was going to jump out of my chest.

I was standing right behind my father as he unlocked the front door. "Sweetie, we're here," he called out.

Donna, my father's wife, stepped out of the kitchen. She looked like the All-American housewife in her apron, which was wrapped around a flowered rayon-looking dress. Her hair was pinned up with several curls dangling loosely.

"Hello, Jasmine," she said, as she wiped her hands on her apron. "You're just in time for dinner." I couldn't make out the look on her face. She was smiling, but it seemed really fake. Before I could figure it out, two girls came barreling down the stairs. They both had long, black ponytails and wore matching short sets. They looked like they were about twelve or thirteen years old. "Daddy," they called out at the same time as they raced to put their arms around his neck.

"How are my babies?" my father asked as he picked both of them up and swung them around. I couldn't help but smile. He still called them his babies. My gaze made its way around their spacious living room. It was a huge, wide-open area. There was a fireplace with pictures all along the mantel. Pictures of my father, Donna, the girls, and a tall, handsome boy who had to be Kevin, all lined up in an array of silver frames.

"Girls," my father said as he put the girls down. "This is your sister, the one I told you about, Jasmine."

The one on the right stuck her hand out, a huge smile across her face. "Hi, I'm Carla." She pointed to her sister, who had lost her excitement and was standing with her arms crossed and a funky look across her face. "This is my twin, Darla. So, are you coming to live with us?"

I smiled widely. "Yes, I am."

"You can't stay in our room," Darla snapped. She and Carla looked exactly alike—even down to the tiny freckles on their butter-colored faces.

I was a little stunned at Darla's nasty attitude. It was obvious she didn't like me and I hadn't even said two words to her. "I hadn't planned on it," I replied.

"Stay outta my way and I'll stay outta yours." Darla turned and spun off before I could say another word. I don't know why she had such a funky attitude with me. She didn't even know me.

"You'll have to excuse my twin," Carla said. "She's not a very friendly person. The total opposite of me."

"Sweetie, why don't you help Jasmine get settled in her room," my father said.

I liked the sound of that. My room. My room and my room only.

Suddenly Darla wasn't the only one giving me the evil eye. Donna was no longer smiling. She was now staring—make that glaring—at me. So much so that it was making me uncomfortable. Still, I tried to be understanding. Here I was, a child she didn't even know about until recently, coming to live with her.

Upstairs, Carla showed me my room and helped me unpack the two big suitcases I'd brought with me.

"I love having a twin, but I've always wondered what it would be like to have an older sister," Carla said as she stretched out across my bed. "I hope you're cool. Kevin never wants to be bothered with me."

I pulled my suitcase up on the bed and opened it. "I think I'm pretty cool," I said, as I started removing stuff from my suitcase. "I'd love kickin' it with you."

"Just a word of warning. Mama doesn't like for us to use slang around her," Carla said.

I frowned but made a mental note to watch my words.

Carla and I spent the next hour laughing and talking. It felt good to have someone I could just kick it with and not have to worry about fighting. I liked how she looked up to me. She asked me a hundred and one questions. And she hung on to my every word like I was the smartest person in the world.

My father stuck his head in the door. "Are you ready to eat?"

I nodded and me and Carla followed him downstairs. Darla was already sitting at the table, attitude still written all over her face. Breaking her down was going to be a whole lot harder than Carla.

I sat down at the table, next to Carla. Her sister didn't seem to like that, either. I looked down at a plate of what looked like Brussels sprouts and other leafy plants in front of me. I didn't really like salads before dinner but I guess I wouldn't protest.

Darla leaned in and whispered, "Get used to it. My mom's a vegetarian. So that means we all are. Enjoy your dinner." She snickered.

I stared at my plate. Vegetarian? As in no meat? This was my meal?

Carla noticed my expression and tried to stifle her laughter. "Don't worry, Darla and I are always sneaking off to go get a burger," she whispered.

Donna walked in and must've noticed the look on my face, too. "I hope you don't have a problem with vegetarian foods?" she said as she placed another plant-looking dish on the table.

"Umm, no ma'am. I don't have a problem with it." I picked up my fork.

"Besides, you probably could benefit from some vegetarian meals," she said as she reached down and patted my thigh. Darla laughed and I tried not to let my embarrassment show.

I leaned over and dug into my food. Donna loudly cleared her throat as she took her seat across the table. "I don't know what you're used to, Jasmine, but around here we say grace before a morsel of food goes in our mouths," she said.

"Sorry," I said as I placed my fork down. Donna looked at my dad, who had just sat down at the head of the table. He immediately reached out and grabbed her hand. Me, Darla, and Carla followed suit.

Donna lowered her head. "Heavenly Father, we ask that You bless this food as it provides nourishment for our souls. Father, we also ask that you forgive my husband again for what he has done to this family and for making me relive that terrible, terrible time in my life."

My eyes popped open. Everyone else still had their eyes closed. I closed mine again.

"Father, we come to You today asking for strength as we bring this stranger into our home," she continued.

Okay, she was straight trippin'. I looked around again. No one seemed fazed by this odd prayer.

"And Lord," she continued. "Let our punishment serve as a testimony to my husband's remorse. These and other blessings we ask in Your name. Amen."

"Amen," everyone but me said. I looked around trying to make sense of what that was all about.

It really bugged me for a minute, but eventually I just let it drop since everyone seemed to have moved on and was making idle chatter during dinner.

"Hey, Dad, Jasmine is going to a basketball banquet this weekend with her boyfriend. She doesn't have anything to wear and needs us to buy her a dress," Carla threw out. I almost choked on my food. I had told Carla about my date with Donovan, but I never expected her to tell my father. I had planned to wait a couple of days before bringing that up.

"Mmph," Donna muttered as she turned her lips down. "Been here less than an hour and already asking for stuff."

"Donna," my father chastised.

I didn't want them thinking that I was only interested in their money. "Oh, no. I . . . I have some money saved. I was going to buy my own dress," I lied. I only had fifty bucks to my name. And that wouldn't get me anything decent.

"Well, first of all," Donna said, "we're not sure about this date thing, period. In this house, young ladies don't date until they turn eighteen."

Eighteen! I'd be dang near out of high school by then. And the dance was a week away. I couldn't back out on Donovan now.

My father must've noticed the look of horror on my face. "Well, I'm sure we can make an exception on this since Jasmine didn't know the rules prior to making this date."

Donna shook her head, obviously getting upset. "Make an exception for one, you have to make an exception for them all. Carla, how about you? You got anybody you want to go out with?"

Carla's eyes lit up. "Yeah! This boy named Lamar at my school."

"Great! Set it up. What about you, Darla? You wanna find some boy to take you out of town for the weekend? Since we're letting you girls do what you want to do these days, why not go for it." Donna threw up her hands in disgust.

"Donna, please. Can we talk about this later?" my father said.

"What is there to talk about? You've decided it. So she gets to go on her date. Just like you've decided everything else in the last three weeks." Donna pushed back from the table, stood up, and started gathering up dishes. I sat with my mouth hanging open. The last thing I wanted to do was cause problems.

"You'll have to excuse Donna," my father said as she

walked out of the dining room. "She's still a little upset about this . . . this whole situation. She'll come around."

My father took a sip of his iced tea. I thought my mom could act a fool. But Donna was out of order. And after that fiasco, I definitely would have to find another way to get a new dress to wear to the banquet because there was no way I was going to ask them now.

23

I was tired and bummed out. Tired because that drive from LaMarque to the church and back was kicking my butt. And bummed out because I couldn't stop thinking about how Donna was trippin'.

"That woman is psycho," Camille said, shaking her head. I had just finished filling everyone in on Donna's prayer, her constant little comments, and her obvious hate for me.

"Yeah, she's being a total witch to you," Angel said.

Trina rolled her eyes. "She ain't being a witch, she's being a—" She bit her lip just as Rachel walked in the room.

"I just know you were not about to use any foul language up here in the house of the Lord," Rachel said.

"Of course not, Miss Rachel," Trina grinned.

"Umm-hmm," Rachel said. "I see y'all started the meeting without me."

"We were just talking about Jasmine's dad," Trina said. "His wife is totally trippin' with her."

"You see, all that glitters isn't gold," Rachel said as she shook her head and got situated at the table at the front.

"My dad isn't that bad," Jasmine said.

"Well, what about the banquet? Are they going to let you go?" Trina said.

"You really think they won't let you go?" Alexis asked.

I shrugged. "Naw, it looks like I'll be able to go. But Donna isn't happy about it. And she definitely isn't about to buy me a new dress."

"Well, you'll just have to wear something you already have," Rachel said.

Trina shot me a look. I knew what she was thinking: that I better get off my high horse and do what I needed to do to get a new dress. Because Tori was waiting in the wings to get my man.

"Oh, shoot, I forgot the article I wanted to show you all in my office. I'll be right back," Rachel said, rushing out of the door.

As soon as she stepped away, Trina turned to me. "You know the cheerleaders go to the banquet. And you'd better believe Tori is bringing her A game. You can't walk up in there in some hand-me-downs."

I sighed. "I know." I looked around the room at Alexis, Camille, and Angel. "I don't want to, but at this point, I have no other choice." I looked down at the floor, then back up at Trina. "So, when can we go to the mall?"

I felt bad. I'd tried to do right, but right wasn't working. Now I had to do what I had to do. And anyone who didn't understand that, well, that was just too bad.

I didn't know what I was thinking bringing Carla along, but she had been bugging to go with me since she found out I was going to the mall. I tried to get out of it by saying I didn't want to drive with her in the car all the way back to Houston since we were going to Memorial City Mall. When that didn't work, I'd tried to tell her I was doing some work with the Good Girlz, but Donna had insisted that I take her. I suspected that Donna thought I was trying to sneak off and see a boy or something and wanted Carla to tag along just in case.

I almost told Trina and Alexis I couldn't go through with it because I didn't want Carla to figure out what was going on, but the banquet was tonight. I was kicking myself for waiting 'til the last minute but Donna had me working like Cinderella all week long. And she was ten times worse than my grandmother, because her stuff had to be spotless. I scrubbed and washed and mopped until I thought I was going to lose my mind. At least she had *all* of us cleaning like that, my father included. It was crazy, but Darla and Carla seemed like they were used to it.

I looked around the store. I was scared to death. Trina made it seem so easy. I had watched as she stuffed dresses, jeans, and a few blouses into a bag. But this was different. Now it was my turn to actually take something, and I wanted to run up out of the store, and forget I had ever agreed to do this in the first place.

Trina had been adamant that if I wanted the dress I had to help. She said she couldn't be taking all the risks by herself, which I thought was strange because she always seemed to get off on taking the stuff. Personally, I think she was just in a foul mood today or something.

Me, Trina, and Alexis had barely gotten in the door good when the sales associate walked up to us.

"May I help you find something?"

"Ummm, no thanks. I'm fine," I replied, trying to play it cool.

"Well, I'm Damali. If you need anything, just let me know."

I nodded as she shot me a smile and walked off. I tried to calm my nerves as I sent Carla to get us some smoothies. We made our way on into the store. We spotted *the dress* right away—an absolutely gorgeous hunter green long dress that not only was going to have Donovan's mouth wide open, but every other boy in the place as well. Camille was meeting me at my dad's to do my hair later this afternoon. I think she and Angel were even more excited than I was.

When Damali walked in the back, I thought we were in the clear. Trina came and stood behind me, and I blocked her from the view from the front of the store. I felt my hands shaking even though Trina was the one with the wire cutters. I felt a thin strip of perspiration on my forehead, and I had long ago stopped trying to control my heart. It was pounding away so fast, I kept looking around to make sure others couldn't hear it.

Alexis went back and started talking with the clerk who was working the register to try and keep her distracted. In one sweeping move Trina snipped the wires that held the dress to the security sensor and folded it. Within seconds the dress was in my foil-lined bag and I had moved on to look at a rack of sweaters. Trina didn't follow me. She walked over to Damali, who was coming out of the back, and started asking her a question.

I couldn't believe just how easy it had all been. I couldn't get out of that store fast enough. Carla walked up just as

Alexis and I were heading to the door. She stopped us and handed me my smoothie.

"I got you strawberry-banana," she said.

Trina looked at me as she rushed out of the store. "Let's go."

She didn't have to tell me twice. I grabbed the smoothie, clutched the bag tighter, and walked out the store. But as soon as I stepped foot back into the mall, I heard a voice I'll never forget for the rest of my entire life.

"Um, excuse me, ladies," the man said. He had a deep, scary voice. It was so casual, no kind of urgency whatsoever. We all stopped and stared at him.

It wasn't until we were surrounded by three uniformed security officers that it dawned on me.

"We're gonna have to ask y'all to come with us," one of the uniforms said.

My eyes searched Trina's for guidance, but she looked like she didn't know what to do, either. Alexis looked just as confused. When one of the guards took Trina by the arm and she pulled away, I thought we might run. But I think all of us were too stunned to try it. I decided to try and play it cool.

We were escorted back to a small security office. No one spoke. Carla kept looking at me, her eyes begging me to tell her what was going on. I just kept thinking that I should have worn something old or borrowed something from Nikki. I didn't know what I was going to do.

"We need to empty all of those bags, and we need you"—the officer who was doing all the talking pointed at Trina—"to take everything out of your top and empty your purse." He turned to another officer. "Call Bianca for a search," he ordered. He looked down at a clipboard, then back up again. "Then call the police."

"You guys are arresting us?" I asked. "We didn't do anything." Why was I lying when the evidence was right there in my bag?

"Shut up!" Trina snapped at me.

"What do you expect when you shoplift? We convict all thieves," he said coldly and turned his attention back to his clipboard.

I knew it was just a matter of time before they told us we could make our one phone call. Who in the world would I call? My mother, who would go ballistic, or my father, who would no doubt tell Donna? It was the lesser of two evils. No, thank you. I'd use my one call to call Donovan and break the news that it looked like I wouldn't be able to make it to the banquet.

24

I sat at the table, still trying to make sense of how I'd ended up downtown at the Houston Police Department. Carla sat across from me, a terrified look on her face. Alexis was leaned up against the table in the stale-smelling office. The office walls were bare, with the exception of an old Houston Astros poster on the wall.

I was still so upset that I couldn't even talk. Donovan had been crushed and all but begged me for an explanation. I had told him my father wouldn't let me go, but I knew he didn't believe me. Especially because he begged to talk to my father and I just hung up the phone on him. I had to before I broke down crying.

Alexis had muttered "I'm so sorry" as we made our way out the mall in handcuffs. But other than that, she hadn't said two words to me. Probably because she knew better.

If I wasn't surrounded by cops, I'd probably be beating Alexis down right now. Trina was lucky they'd taken her to another room because, as it turned out, this was her third offense. Not to mention that she had another outfit in her purse. That was how they'd gotten hip to us. Trina had gotten greedy and security spotted her stuffing a blouse and skirt in her oversize purse.

Since it was me, Carla, and Alexis's first time being arrested, they told us to just wait in this room.

I rolled my eyes for the millionth time and shifted in my seat. I turned my head as the office door opened. My eyes lit up at the sight of Rachel, who eyed us disapprovingly. "Thank you so much for letting me in to talk to them," she told the officer.

"No problem, Rachel. When they told me they were with your group, I thought I'd give you a call. I think that Good Girlz program is an awesome thing you've got going," the female officer said.

"Thank you, Lydia. And I guess it helps to know people in high places," Rachel responded.

"Please, I've been at Zion Hill as long as you have." The officer looked at us and shook her head. "You can have a minute to talk to them before their parents get here."

I wanted to die at the mention of my mother. The officer had called her after they couldn't get my father. Donna was on her way as well. Just thinking about my mother and Donna, I figured I'd be better off if they just put me under the jail.

Rachel pulled up a chair to the table as the officer closed the door behind her. "I know you two are about to tell me this is all a big misunderstanding. I just know you were not somewhere stealing." She sat down and I felt my heart drop at the disappointed look on her face.

"Is somebody going to answer me?" Rachel asked. Alexis lowered her eyes and stared at the floor. I glared at Alexis. She hadn't made me take that dress, but she was the one who got us caught up in this madness in the first place.

Rachel shook her head. "Then you got this child here caught up in all of this," she said, pointing to Carla. "Are you okay?"

Carla nodded, but still looked terrified. "I didn't know nothing about this."

Rachel squeezed her hand before turning back to me and Alexis. "You might want to tell me what's going on before your parents get here. At least maybe then I can help get you out of trouble."

The door swung open again. Alexis looked away at the sight of her father standing there looking agitated.

I groaned at the sight of my mother standing behind Alexis's father. Her look was more than just agitated. It was downright furious. She still had on her housekeeper uniform, which meant she had come straight from work, or worse, been called off her job.

Rachel stood as they entered. "Hi, Jetola," she said to my mother, whom she knew from back when she used to babysit me. Rachel turned to Alexis's father. "You must be Mr. Lansing," Rachel said as she extended her hand. He shook it, but didn't take his eyes off Alexis.

"Sit down, both of you," Rachel said. "You two know I work with the county through the Good Girlz group so the officers are letting me deal with this. But Alexis and Jasmine are in a lot of trouble."

"Would you just tell us what happened," my mother snapped. Both she and Mr. Lansing were still standing.

"They were caught shoplifting," Rachel said.

My mother took two steps toward me like she was about to knock me upside my head.

"Jetola," Rachel said, grabbing her arm. "Please, don't

do that here. We're trying to handle this ourselves and we don't want the police coming in here."

"I know this little girl was not somewhere stealing! I didn't raise no thief!" my mother snapped. Then she noticed Carla and said, "Who is that?"

"That's Carla," Rachel replied.

"Franklin's daughter?" my mother said.

Carla nodded.

"Please tell me you do not have her caught up in this."

I couldn't respond, especially when Carla started crying. At that moment, the female officer poked her head in the door. "You can come with me," she said, pointing at Carla.

Carla quickly got up and followed the officer out. She didn't even look at me as she left.

Donna was going to kill me. After my mom got through killing me. I couldn't believe I'd been so stupid.

Alexis's father finally spoke. "Alexis, do you want to tell me what's going on? I had to leave a very important business meeting to come down here for this nonsense. Your mother isn't answering her cell phone. I really do not have time to deal with what must be a big misunderstanding. I could buy that department store, so you couldn't possibly have any reason to be stealing anything out of there."

Alexis bit her lip but didn't say anything.

My mother stepped up. "Oh my goodness, you're Arthur Lansing from the Lansing Hotels?"

"Yes, that's me."

My mother suddenly seemed aware that she was acting a fool, standing there in her uniform because she raised her hand and brushed down her hair. "Please, let me offer my apologies," she said, her voice suddenly sounding a lot more proper. "I'm sure this is all my daughter's fault." She glared at me. "She's been in a lot of trouble lately, and I just don't know what to do about her."

I jumped up. "What? You're kidding me, right?"

"Sit down and shut up," my mother hissed. She turned back toward Alexis's father. "You know how teenagers are—sometimes they can be led down the wrong path easily."

"Yeah, and Alexis was the one doing the leading!" I screamed.

Rachel reached out and touched my arm. "Please, Jasmine, I need you to calm down."

My mother turned her attention back to me. "It's bad enough I'm losing money because I have to come down here for this. Now you're dragging this sweet child into your troubles," she said, as she pointed at Alexis. "And Carla!"

Mr. Lansing stared at Alexis, shaking his head. "I do not believe you. You are on punishment and are not to leave your room for a month."

"It's not like you're even there to make sure I stick to my punishment," Alexis mumbled.

He took a deep breath. "I do not have time for your smart mouth." He looked at his watch. "Rachel, is there anything else that needs to be done? Are they going to press charges?"

"No, since it's Alexis and Jasmine's first offense. The store manager believes the girls were only accessories, so he won't press charges as long as the dress is paid for," Rachel replied.

"How much is it?"

"One hundred seventy dollars," Rachel said.

"One hundred seventy dollars?" my mother yelled, then caught herself and lowered her voice. "I mean, that's absurd."

"It sure is," Alexis's father said as he pulled out his wallet. "Especially considering you have a freaking twenty-thousand-dollar limit on your credit card," he snapped at Alexis.

Everyone's eyes got wide when he said that. Alexis didn't seem fazed.

"Can you handle this?" Alexis's father asked my mother. "I really must get back to the hotel. I have some important clients from China in town."

"Of course," my mother replied. I rolled my eyes. My mother looked like an idiot over there batting her eyelids at that man. Like he would ever want someone like her.

"Thank you so much," he said as he handed her four one-hundred-dollar bills and a business card. "Please use this to pay the store manager. Please also give him my business card and tell him to call my secretary to book a weekend at one of my hotels. On me, of course. The other hundred is for your troubles in dealing with this because Lord knows I don't have time."

"Of course," my mother said again as she stared at the money in her hand. You'd think she'd never seen a hundred dollars before the way she was standing there in awe.

Mr. Lansing shot Alexis one last disappointed glance before turning and hurrying out of the room.

"Come on, Jetola. I'll take you down to try and get things squared away with the store manager. He's in my friend's office," Rachel said. I cringed as my mother shot me a look to let me know I was still in a world of trouble. She followed Rachel out of the room.

"Thanks a lot for getting me involved in all of this, Alexis," I snapped as I plopped down in the chair.

"I'm really sorry." Alexis looked like she wanted to cry. "I'm in trouble, too," she said softly.

I looked at her like she was crazy. "You can't leave your room. You have a phone, a computer, a TV, a DVD player, a stereo, and every CD under the sun. What kind of punishment is that?"

Alexis wiped her face. "At least your mother cares. My father did what he always does, tossed some money to make his headaches go away." She seemed like she was talking to herself. "Not even stealing can get his attention," she muttered.

"What is that supposed to mean?" I asked.

Alexis shook her head. "Nothing, just forget it. You may think your mom is crazy, but you need to count your blessings."

"Are you on crack?" I said. "You just saw my mom in here acting a fool. I'm supposed to count my blessing for that?"

"Like I said, at least she cares." Alexis turned her head and stared at the blank wall.

Had she done this just to get attention? Was her home life that bad that she would go to these lengths just to get her father to care? That was messed up that her daddy acted like she wasn't nothing but a big inconvenience.

I couldn't believe it, but I actually felt sorry for Alexis.

25

I wasn't sure if I was headed back to my mother's or if she was actually going to take me back to my father's house. She hadn't said two words to me since we left the police station. Normally, I would've thought that was a good thing, but her silence was even more frightening than her yelling.

My questions were answered as she navigated her beat-up old Ford Taurus onto Highway 45 and started heading south toward La Marque.

After about fifteen minutes of silence, I finally said something. "Mama, I'm sor—"

She held up her hand. "Don't. Do not say anything to me."

So I just leaned back in the seat and rode the rest of the way in silence.

When we pulled up in front of my father's house, which I was surprised she even knew where it was, my mother threw the car in park and waited for me to get out.

"Mama," I tried one more time. She cut me off again, and waved me out of the car.

"Good-bye, Jasmine. Let your father deal with you now."

My father must've been looking out the window because the door flew open and he came barreling down the sidewalk with anger all over his face.

I turned toward him and stood frozen for a moment. He had a look I had never seen before.

"I cannot believe you are a thief!" he yelled.

I looked back at my mother. I could've sworn I saw she was crying as she sped off.

"Do I need to lock up my belongings? I can't believe you got my daughter caught up in your thievery." He grabbed me and shook me and I swear I'd never been more scared in my life.

I was shaking. "I'm sorry."

"Sorry? Is that the best you can do?" He took a deep breath and pushed me inside so hard I almost fell. "Get inside before someone sees you."

I caught my balance then scurried inside, shocked because this man was not the same person I'd come to know over the last few weeks. When I walked inside, Donna was standing in the living room. She flashed a hateful look at me before turning and walking back into the kitchen.

I made my way upstairs, not sure of what I should do. I wanted to check on Carla and was actually heading to the twins' room when the hall bathroom door swung open.

"Get away from my door, you klepto," Darla snapped. She stomped past me, rolling her eyes. "Carla hasn't ever been in trouble. You come here messing everything up. Stay away from me. Stay away from my sister. Why don't you go back to wherever you came from!" She slammed her bedroom door in my face.

I stood in the hallway for a minute before making my way on to my room. It was well after eleven o'clock. My mind went to Donovan. I hated that I couldn't go with him, hated that I had stuck him out like that to go to the banquet alone. I was hoping he'd calm down in a couple of days. But I was really bummed about not seeing him get his award. I couldn't believe I had caused so much trouble over a stupid dress.

I waited around in my room for almost thirty minutes before hunger got the best of me. I eased open my door and made my way back downstairs. I stopped right outside the kitchen door when I heard my father and Donna arguing.

"You bring your little hood rat into my home and what does she do? Corrupt my child!" Donna yelled.

"Donna, I have apologized a thousand times. I had no way of knowing she was a thief."

"What did you expect? Her mother is a ghetto home-wrecker and the apple doesn't fall too far from the tree. Now I have to lock up all my belongings because if she'll steal from the store, she'll steal from us. She's probably on drugs, too. The police will come here and find drugs in her room and we'll all get arrested."

I fought back tears. I prayed my father would come to my defense. I knew he didn't know me that well, but he had to know I'd just made a big mistake. I wasn't a thief.

"Carla could be scarred for life having to sit down there at that police station," Donna continued. "She cried all the way home." I heard her slamming cabinet doors. "You know, it's bad enough I had to deal with you cheating on me, but then you come here sixteen years later with a *reminder* that you cheated on me. You have this bright idea to bring her here to atone for your sins and look what happens!"

My father's voice sounded dejected. "I'm just trying to finally do right."

"Well, now we all are suffering from your actions. Again. Send her back. I don't want her in my house."

"Donna . . ." my father said.

"Don't *Donna* me. I went along with this cockamamie idea to bring her here even though I was totally against it. Newspaper and TV reporters are calling here, for Christ's sake. Everybody wants to know about the superintendent's illegitimate shoplifting child."

I felt like I was going to pass out. It had always been obvious Donna didn't like me, but I had no idea she hated me that much.

"Look, Franklin," Donna continued. She took a deep breath like she was trying really hard to get through to my father. "Jetola might not have taken the money to get rid of the baby, but when I took you back, you agreed to sever all ties with her. Now you come to me sixteen years later, letting guilt overcome you, talking about righting wrongs. But this is too much. She has to go."

What? What in the world was she talking about? My father hadn't known I existed. I couldn't help it. I could no longer hold my silence. I pushed the door open and stood in the entryway.

"You lied to me?"

My father stared at me like he had no idea what to say.

"You knew about me?" I asked.

My father put his hand to his head and rubbed his

temple. I turned toward Donna. "And you made him disown me?"

Donna just looked at me.

I was dumbfounded as I looked back and forth between her and my father. "Daddy, this isn't making any sense."

"Sit down, baby." My father had tears in his eyes as I sat across from him.

"Just tell her the truth. Tell her, then send her home," Donna hissed.

I glared at my stepmother. My grandma used to always say that you shouldn't hate people. The emotion was too strong. But at that very moment, I hated Donna. How could someone be so mean and cruel?

"Donna, please let me handle this," my father pleaded.

"No. I let you handle it sixteen years ago and look what happened." Donna sat down next to my father. "Your father had an affair. You are the product of that affair. You can tell me I'm wrong, but the only way our family could heal from that was for your father to pretend it never happened."

"But I *did* happen," I protested.

Donna ignored my protest and continued talking. "Your mother wouldn't take the money we offered her to disappear or deal with the problem, but I assured her that we would have no part in your life. She accepted that, so you can't blame us. Blame her."

I looked at my father. "And you went along with all this?" When he didn't say anything, the tears I had been holding back came falling down. "You—you said you didn't know about me."

"Oh, he knew all right," Donna said. I couldn't believe she was being so hateful.

"Let me explain," my father said.

"Explain what?" I stood up, stunned. "You lied."

"Jasmine, sit back down so we can talk."

Donna huffed, scooted her chair away from the table, then stormed out of the room.

"You'll have to excuse her," he said. I eased into a chair across from him, recalling how many times he'd said that since I came here. "I hurt her really bad and I think this is just years' worth of anger coming out."

I didn't even care about Donna at that point. "You've known about me all these years?"

"It's more complicated than that. I . . . I had just built this life and I knew . . . Donna . . . and Kevin . . . my career . . . I knew it would just be hard on everyone." He shook his head from side to side. "Donna is just—she can be so overbearing. And I wanted to do right by her. I knew it was wrong, but it was the only way I could keep my family intact."

I could only stare at him in disbelief. "I'm your family, too."

"I know. I don't expect you to understand."

I wiped my face. Good thing he wasn't expecting me to understand because I definitely didn't. "Why did you let me come live with you?"

My father shook his head. "Guilt? I don't know. I think my guilt just got the best of me."

"Guilt? I thought you were so happy to find me. I thought you loved me."

"I do love you . . ."

"Stop it. You don't even know me." My grandmother's words flashed in my mind: *Sometimes our blessings are disguised—what we don't think is a blessing, is; what we think is a blessing, isn't.* It finally made sense. "I am so stupid," I whispered.

"Jasmine, don't do this."

I wiped my tears. I didn't think I'd ever felt as much pain as I felt at that very moment.

"Do you want me to leave?" I stared at him.

"I . . ." My father stopped talking and looked past me. I turned to see Donna back in the doorway. She was glaring at him but didn't say anything. He turned his attention back to me.

"I think it would be best. I'm sorry, Jasmine. It's just not working. But we can stay in touch."

I turned to walk out. "I'll go pack my stuff."

"Jasmine, please don't be mad. Try to understand."

I spun around, still trying to fight back the tears. "Understand what? That you didn't *want* to see me? That you just wanted to pretend I didn't exist 'cause your wife said so? That you're abandoning me again? I can't understand that."

I raced upstairs to call my mother. I didn't think twice when I dialed her number. I breathed a sigh of relief when she picked up the phone.

"Mama?"

She hesitated. "Yeah?"

"Can I come home?"

"I'm on my way to get you." I was shocked that she didn't ask any questions or chastise me. In fact, she seemed relieved. "And Jasmine?"

"Yes, Mama?"

"I love you."

I released the waterfall of tears that I had been fighting back. "I love you, too, Mama."

I put the phone back on the hook and went to pack my bags.

26

I threw my book bag into my locker as I thought about my conversation with my mom yesterday. She was still upset about the shoplifting. But she was so happy to have me back home. And honestly, I was happy to be back. I never in a million years thought I'd say that. But after my experience with my dad, I'd take my mom any day.

Of course, my grandmother and my brothers were happy to see me. Even Nikki hugged me.

I hadn't talked to Donovan. He wouldn't answer my calls. I'd blown up his cell phone all day yesterday and he still didn't call me back. I guess he was still mad. I couldn't wait to find him and beg him to forgive me.

I slammed my locker door shut and made my way down Hall B, toward Donovan's locker.

I had just rounded the corner when I saw something that stopped me in my tracks.

"Please tell me I'm not seeing what I think I'm seeing," I mumbled to myself.

Tori was draped all over my man once again. This time, though, he was grinning back. They were standing next to each other at his locker. I didn't know whether to be mad or cry.

I walked over to Donovan without looking at Tori. "What's going on, Donovan?"

He immediately dropped his arm, which had been leaned against the locker. "H-Hey Jasmine."

Tori looked at me like she was the girlfriend and I was the one trying to push up on her man. "Excuse me, we were having a private conversation," she said.

It was my turn to look at her crazy. "You got me messed up."

Tori rolled her eyes and adjusted her purse on her shoulder. "I have to get to class, Donovan." She rubbed his arm gently and flashed him a smile. "I had a really good time at the banquet. Thank you so much for taking me." She cut her eyes at me, then walked off. If I wasn't so stunned I would've snatched her back by her hair.

Donovan lowered his eyes.

"You took her to the banquet?" I was floored. I just knew he was going to tell me Tori was just trying to make me jealous. "Answer me, Donovan. Did you take her to the banquet?" I asked, raising my voice.

He looked around like he was worried about someone overhearing us. "Jasmine, what did you expect me to do? I was supposed to sit at the head table and you bailed on me with some lie about your dad not letting you go. You couldn't even get your lie out good. I mean, I couldn't go without a date. I would've been the only one there who didn't have one."

I looked at him, my eyes full of fury. "But Tori, of all people?"

"I'm sorry. I just didn't want to go alone," he said. "When I told Levi you had left me stuck out, he called Tori since he knew she was going. She offered to be my date."

"I'll just bet she did," I snapped.

Donovan sighed. "Look, Jasmine, there's nothing goin' on with me and Tori."

"That didn't look like nothing I just walked up on," I yelled.

"Would you lower your voice? I don't want people all up in my business."

"I don't care about people. I care about the fact that you cheated on me!"

"Didn't nobody cheat on you," Donovan said with a sigh.

I flicked my hand at him. "Whatever, Donovan. I thought you were better than that. You're just a no-good dog."

Donovan cocked his head. "Oh, so I'm a no-good dog? You stood *me* up. On one of the most important days of my life, you were a no-show. Yeah, I took Tori to the banquet, then I took her home. She didn't want to go home. She wanted to go to a motel. But I took her home. Now, with the way you're acting, maybe I should've taken her up on her offer. 'Cuz it ain't like I'm getting none from you no way."

I couldn't believe he'd gone there.

"That was foul, Donovan." I took a deep breath. "But you know, if you want to make it like that, then fine. Go get it from Tori. Just get in line because everybody at school done had her." I turned and stormed off.

Camille caught up with me just as I pushed through the doors out onto the courtyard.

"Jasmine, what's going on? I saw you going off on Donovan. Tori made it a point to tell me she was with him now and you were over there acting a fool."

I stopped and spun around. "Forget Donovan. Forget Tori." I raised my arms in disgust and noticed my bangle bracelets. I snatched them off my arm and threw them on the ground. "Forget this stupid jewelry." I pulled my hair back and twisted a piece around to form a ponytail. "Forget this whole stupid transformation thing. Because in the end, it didn't mean nothing!" I stormed off to my class, ignoring the sounds of Camille calling my name.

27

What was I thinking, coming to the meeting today? This was our first meeting since the arrest. And after the last couple of days I'd had, I was in no mood to hear a lecture from Rachel.

Me and Donovan were officially over. Tori made sure of that. And it was like she was glued to him because he couldn't take two steps without her all up in his grill. I couldn't stand neither one of them.

Rachel walked into the room. "Well, hello," she said to me and Alexis in particular. "I think we have a lot to talk about."

I groaned and Alexis lowered her head in shame.

"Which one of you wants to tell me what happened? From start to finish," she said. Angel and Camille, who were sitting in front of us, didn't say a word. Of course, Alexis had filled them in on what happened. And I'd answered a hundred and one questions myself.

"So, I guess you all are taking the 'don't snitch' policy? Well, that's what got you into trouble in the first place." Rachel sighed and sat down on a chair in the first row. "Do you know that Trina is going to jail?"

"We know. She was arrested with us," Alexis said.

Rachel shook her head. "No, to jail for real. For a while. She's being tried as an adult. They found a bunch of other stolen items in her home. This isn't her first offense so the district attorney plans to throw the book at her. Do you know what that means?"

We shook our heads.

"It means she can go to prison. With hard-core prisoners."

We all wore stunned looks. I had halfway come to care about Trina and I didn't want to see her go to jail.

"Trina will never make it in prison," Alexis all but whispered.

"Well, it looks like she will have to find a way," Rachel said. She shifted in her seat and directed her attention at me and Alexis. "You know what you did could have really landed you behind bars?"

We both nodded.

She turned to Camille and Angel. "Did you two know about this?" They both stared blankly at Rachel without saying anything.

"You knew? Please don't tell me you were part of this little scheme?" Rachel stood up when they still didn't respond. "Are we not learning anything in the Good Girlz? I mean, are we meeting for our health?" She took a deep breath, obviously trying to calm down. "I can't believe you girls," she added.

"Miss Rachel, it's not like *we* actually stole anything," Angel said.

"Yeah," Camille added. "I never took a thing."

"And? You think that makes you any less guilty? You

knew the stuff was stolen and you didn't tell a soul. You're deceiving yourself if you think you're not just as guilty. What did you need all this stuff for anyway?" she asked, turning back to me and Alexis.

I contemplated lying. But I was sick of lying and stealing. "Alexis and Trina sold it."

"Oh my," Rachel said. "You had a business?" Alexis nodded. Rachel rubbed her forehead. "Okay, legalities aside, did you ever give any thought to how God would feel about what you were doing? I mean, right there in the Ten Commandments, big as day, it says, thou shalt not steal."

All of us looked at each other.

"We didn't think it was that big of a deal because like Alexis said, all those stores have insurance," Angel said softly.

Rachel shook her head.

"We didn't really think about it at all," Alexis added.

"I'm going to say something you all already know. You just chose to tailor it to your own definition," Rachel said. "Stealing is wrong, no matter how you slice it. Whether you take something yourself, receive the stolen items, or simply know about it and don't say anything about it—it's wrong. In the eyes of the law, it's wrong. And in God's eyes, it's wrong. Do you all understand me?"

Everyone in the room nodded.

"Consider yourselves lucky. No, let me correct that," Rachel passed and gave us a hard glare. "Consider yourselves blessed that the store manager didn't press charges. You could have had your lives ruined over some *clothes*. It wasn't worth it. It wasn't even worth taking that chance."

There was nothing any of us could say. We knew Rachel was right.

Rachel sighed heavily. "But don't think just because you got off with the police, you got off with me. Part of my agreement in convincing the store manager not to press charges was that I would beef up your community service. So, instead of one project every other month, we will now do two every month. And they are mandatory. We're starting this Saturday by going to the senior citizens' home and doing some spring cleaning. We will meet here at seven A.M."

I knew everyone had to fight back groans. Not only were we having to be somewhere on the weekend at seven in the morning, but we had to spend the day cleaning up after old people.

"But, Mrs. Rachel," Camille protested, "the battle of the bands is this Saturday."

"Oh, snap, I forgot about that," Angel said. "Maybe we'll be done in enough time to go."

"What time is the battle of the bands?" Rachel asked.

"Eleven," Camille replied.

"Then it looks like you all won't be there," Rachel said nonchalantly.

"Awww, man," Angel whined. "Everybody is gonna be there."

"You all won't," Rachel said as she gathered up her stuff. "Maybe next time you'll think twice before taking something that doesn't belong to you." She headed toward the door. "I have to get to revival." She stopped, turned, and faced us just before stepping out. "Remember, it's mandatory. No excuses."

"Man, this is messed up," Camille said as Rachel walked out the room.

I closed my eyes. Rachel was right. We needed to be counting our blessings that we were just cleaning a senior citizens' home, and not cell block D. After the nightmare that had been my life for the past two weeks, I was just grateful for a second chance.

28

It was finally here. My sixteenth birthday and I couldn't be more miserable. I mean, stuff was a lot better at home, or maybe it was just my attitude that was better. I was back to fighting with my brothers, and cleaning up and cooking all the time. But I wasn't even complaining. I was just happy to be home. I had to pinch myself because I couldn't believe I just said that.

My mom eased open my bedroom door. "Hey, what are you doing?"

I smiled. "Nothing. Just laying here thinking."

"I hope it's about how wrong what you did was."

I nodded. "I know, Mama. And I'm really sorry."

She looked at me. "I know you are, baby."

I gave my mother a look like an alien had invaded her body.

"I'm sorry, too," she said, looking down.

"For what?"

"I should've told you about your father. At the time, I thought I was doing the right thing." My mother sat down next to me on my bed, and for the first time I saw the weariness in her face.

"I know you're wondering why I didn't tell you." She sighed. "When I met your father I had no idea he was married. It wasn't until after I'd been seeing him for almost six months that I learned the truth. He was separated from his wife. Nikki's father had been dead about eight months and I was really lonely. Franklin was everything I wanted, or everything I thought I wanted in a man." She got a faraway look in her eyes, took a deep breath, and continued.

"When I told him I was pregnant, he responded by telling me he was going back to his wife. I was heartbroken. I still intended for him to be a part of your life, but when I met Donna . . ." My mother paused and laughed. "Boy, I tell you, Donna is crazy with a capital C. I even had to get a restraining order against her. I swore that she would never be around you. She hated me, hated you, and told me on numerous occasions if I had you, she would make our lives miserable. And when Frank went along with her, I just knew it was better off to pretend he was dead. I knew no matter what, I didn't want you around all that."

I couldn't believe my ears. She'd kept me from my father to protect me from Donna's wrath? Suddenly I felt so guilty.

"Mama, I had no idea," I said softly.

"How could you?" My mother slapped her hands on her lap. "But enough with this depressing stuff. I took off today so we could spend the day together."

"You took off from work." I reached over and put my hand to her head. "Are you feeling okay?"

My mother slapped my hand away. "Ha, ha. Very funny. I thought we could all go to CiCi's Pizza."

I groaned. "Mama, I'm too old to celebrate my birthday

at CiCi's. Plus, you know Granny is not going to eat any pizza."

My mother laughed. "You're right. Let's go pick up some Chinese food."

"That sounds good," I said as I jumped off my bed. I couldn't remember the last time I went anywhere with my mother. "Let me throw on another shirt."

"Put on that cute green top I like," she said, referring to one of the few gifts she had ever bought me. "I'll be waiting up front."

"Where is everybody?" I asked after I'd changed and walked out into the living room.

"I think your sister's boyfriend took her and the boys to the store."

"All of 'em?"

"He has his daddy's SUV."

"Oh." The apartment didn't feel the same without their stuff everywhere and them laying out all across the sofa and floor. I smiled as I thought about how happy I was to be back home.

We locked up and headed downstairs to my mother's car. "Oh, baby," my mom said just as I was about to get in the car. "I forgot to pick up this box I ordered. They said they left it right inside by the clubhouse door. Will you run over there and get it for me?"

"Is it my present?"

"It just might be," my mother smiled.

"Ooooh," I said as I took off toward the clubhouse.

I looked around outside the clubhouse wondering why they'd leave the door open when it was after six. I gently pushed the door open. Just as I did the lights flicked on.

"Surprise!" everyone yelled.

I looked around the room in total shock. All of my friends were there—Camille, Angel, Alexis. All my siblings. Several people from school. A couple of my cousins. Even Miss Rachel and her niece, Tameka. I turned around to find my mother standing right behind me.

"Happy Birthday, baby."

I knew I was going to lose it. I hadn't had a birthday party since I was five years old. "Thank you, Mama," I said as I threw my arms around her and squeezed her tightly.

"You need to be thanking me," my grandmother said as she walked up to me. "I'm the one who's been slaving in the kitchen all day cooking up this gumbo."

I hugged my grandmother. "Granny, you told me that gumbo was for the church."

"Well, the Lord lets me lie every now and then, long as it's for a good cause." She chuckled.

I laughed as I made my way through the clubhouse. I hugged a few people, stopped and talked to others before Jaquan's friend, Chris, dragged me out on the dance floor. I started to protest because Chris was a booger bear if I ever seen one. But I decided I would just have a good time tonight and not worry about anything else.

Alexis stopped me right before I got on the dance floor. "Hey, girl. Happy birthday."

"Hey yourself. Thank you. I can't believe all of this."

"Can you believe we kept it a secret? Your mom called us last week."

"What? I was still with my dad then."

"I know, but she said she was still having a party for you. Apparently she'd been planning it for a while."

I looked over at my mom as she talked with some neighbors. I couldn't help but smile.

"Anyway," Alexis said, looking at Chris, "I see your dance partner is getting impatient. You'd better get back to him."

Chris didn't even try to fake a smile as he all but dragged me onto the dance floor.

I'd only planned to dance one song, but when the next one came on, I didn't want to leave the dance floor. I had my eyes closed as I made a slow twirl on the dance floor. "Man, I love this song," I said as I turned back around to Chris. "It's—"

"Your favorite song in the world," Donovan said.

I stopped dancing and looked around for Chris, who didn't look too happy as he danced with Camille on the other side of the dance floor.

"I hope you don't mind. I just couldn't stand watching that boy all up on my girl," Donovan said.

I didn't know how to respond. "Oh, so I'm your girl now?" I said, raising my eyebrows.

"If you wanna be."

"What about Tori?"

"What about her?"

"I thought she was your girl."

Donovan leaned in so close I could feel the heat in his breath. I looked around nervously, hoping my mother wasn't watching. She wasn't. But my grandmother sure was. I backed up a little.

"I never have wanted Tori. I wanted you. You can barely go out on dates and you work my nerves. But I still wanted you."

I suddenly realized we were just standing in the middle of the dance floor, so I started swaying a little bit to the music.

"Want*ed* sounds like past tense to me," I said, finally loosening up.

"Then I *want* to be with you. You know I'm flunking English," he joked.

I laughed.

"I missed you."

"I missed you, too, Donovan. You just don't know the drama I've been through these last few days."

He stopped dancing again. "I know. Angel and Camille filled me in. I'm sorry I wasn't there for you."

My eyes got big. I know my girls didn't sell me out like that and tell him about me getting arrested.

"I know how bad you wanted to have a relationship with your dad. I hate that his wife just up and decided she didn't want you there."

I relaxed as I realized Camille and Angel had only given him part of the story. I should've known they'd have my back. Maybe I'd tell Donovan what really happened one day, but right now, that was a part of my life I'd just rather forget about.

"Yeah, but it brought me and my mom closer," I said.

Donovan smiled that near perfect smile. "As my grandmother always says, sometimes our blessings are disguised and things that are good for us are right there in our face." He stared into my eyes as he said that. It gave me goose bumps.

"That's funny. My grandmother says the same thing," I replied.

"Must be in the grandmother's manual or something," Donovan said as he leaned in closer to kiss me. I closed my eyes and waited for his lips to meet mine. Instead, I felt a cold palm against my face. My eyes shot open to find my grandmother's hand right in the middle of me and Donovan.

"Wanna know what else is in the grandmother's manual?" my grandmother snapped. " 'Thou shall cut any nappy-headed little boys that try to kiss your granddaughter right in front of you.' "

Donovan burst out laughing. And for once, instead of being embarrassed, I laughed right along with him.

Blessings in Disguise

ReShonda Tate Billingsley

Reading Group Guide

Description

Since joining Rachel Jackson's after-school church group, Alexis, Jasmine, Camille, and Angel have become the best of friends. Between mentoring local elementary school girls and spending many a sleepover sharing juicy gossip, these four friends are practically sisters. But when Alexis and Jasmine get caught up in their own problems, will they drag their friends into trouble, too?

Rich girl Alexis has the perfect life, but things aren't always what they seem. While the world outside sees a happy, loving family, Alexis watches as her mother and father grow more distant and cold, leaving her afraid that her parents might file for divorce. Determined to keep her family together, Alexis will do whatever it takes to fix their marriage, even if it means doing something drastic to get their attention.

Meanwhile, Jasmine is used to being the glue that keeps her family together, looking after her siblings and cleaning the house while her mother works back-to-back jobs. Tired of being a babysitter and housekeeper extraordinaire, Jasmine decides to move in with her father. But the change of pace isn't all it's cracked up to be, as she uses her newfound free time to steal a dress for the school dance.

Reading Group Discussion Questions

1. Discuss the different family problems that Jasmine and Alexis face. Which girl faces the more difficult challenges? How do they each search for support?
2. Discuss the evolution of how Jasmine views her father. How does her opinion and understanding of him change

throughout the course of the book? What are the biggest factors influencing the way she thinks about him?

3. Mrs. Lansing made the difficult decision to place her daughter Sharon in a home. She says that she did not have a choice (p. 71), but did she? What were the direct and indirect consequences of her actions? Did others in the Lansing family have a role in her decision-making process?
4. Because her mother works long hours to support them, Jasmine often relies on her extended family network. What specific means of support do her aunt, grandmother, and brothers and sister offer her? What about her friends at Good Girlz?
5. Money and theft are major themes in the story. Do Jasmine and Alexis think of money differently? Do you think it's odd that Alexis, whose family has money, is an instigator in their plot to steal?
6. Is Jasmine's new relationship with Donovan a positive or negative influence on her life? How does the relationship make her think and act differently than she did before?
7. Jasmine's father lies to her about his knowledge of her existence and Jasmine's mother fails to tell her the entire truth. Which is worse? How does each parent's version of the story influence what happens to Jasmine and how she makes decisions?
8. Was Donna Sanders wrong to make her husband choose between her and his newborn daughter? Donna is a religious person—is such an ultimatum a religious approach to the problem?
9. Does Frank Sanders love his daughter Jasmine or does he accept her out of guilt? As an administrator in the school system is he a good role model?

10. Do you think that Trina deserves to go to prison? If not, what would be a just punishment?
11. Many of the characters make very questionable decisions. Which one affected you the most? If you could have one character make a different decision, which would it be?
12. What does the title *Blessings in Disguise* refer to? What are the many blessings Jasmine has throughout the entire story, but fails to see until the end?
13. Is there a concrete lesson to be learned at the end of the story? What is it? Is there more than one lesson? If so, which is more important?

Enhance Your Book Club

1. The Good Girlz is a great way for young people to work together for the betterment of the community. Have your reading group work with a local church or community youth group and lead them in a reading and discussion of *Blessings in Disguise.*
2. Because of Hurricane Katrina, Donovan had to move to the Houston area for school. Work with your reading group to donate to the Red Cross at redcross.org or find other methods to support the gulf coast recovery effort.
3. Feeling creative? Have a group member draw a sketch for every major scene in the book. Before you know it you'll have your very own comic book!

A Conversation with ReShonda Tate Billingsley:

1. Growing up, were you a member of a group like the Good Girlz?

   I wasn't, but I wish that I was. I did have a core

group of friends that I could count on to have my back. I think, especially in your teens, having that bond with your friends is wonderful.

2. Authors often remark that they put a little bit of themselves into their characters. Do you identify with any of your characters? Who were your inspirations for Jasmine and Alexis?

   Do I ever! I used to think my mom was the meanest person in the world. I don't have a problem admitting that now, because I so appreciate her now for those very things I couldn't stand growing up. All of my characters are inspired by myself, my friends, my relatives. I took bits and pieces of several people to create them.

3. Both Alexis' and Jasmine's families are key parts to your novel. Why did you choose to tell the story from Jasmine's point of view?

   I wanted Book 2 to be Jasmine's story. While all of the girls have problems, Jasmine's was a bit more complex. I think a lot of people can relate to wanting a different life growing up. I wanted to hammer home the point that all that glitters ain't gold.

4. Your writing career has been enormously diverse, with both fiction and nonfiction books. What do you like to write best, and why? Do you have a favorite book that you have written?

   I absolutely love writing. But I have to admit I enjoy fiction more. I just wanna make stuff up! I think because my day job (I'm a television news reporter) requires that I stick to the facts, I love the ability to escape to a world where I can make my characters say and do whatever I want them to say and do. As for a favorite book—that's like asking a mother to pick her favorite child!! (lol). I really do love them

all. I had so much fun creating characters that it's really hard to say which one I like the best.

5. Faith and moral living play a large role in much of your writing. As a writer, why are these important themes for you?
Absolutely. While I write to entertain, I also want to inspire. I want to help people make good choices in their own lives. I want people to see that it's okay to fall. All that matters is how you pick yourself up and keep going.
6. What made you think of a series with each book having one of the Ten Commandments as its theme?
It was again, all about inspiring young readers. I wanted to teach a strong biblical message without sounding too "preachy." And I wanted to take an everyday issue and relate it to one of the Ten Commandments. I'm pleased with how it turned out.
7. Previously you were a professor at Langston University. What similarities and differences have you found between teaching and writing? Which do prefer?
One of the things I loved about teaching was playing a role in the shaping of young minds. As a professor I was able to help direct and change lives. I had students who had no idea what they wanted to do with their lives and, after my class, not only did they know what they wanted to do—they did it. That means the world to me. And I love being able to have that same effect through writing. I love them both because they each provide a sort of personal enjoyment and fulfillment.
8. What other writers do you like to read? Which authors influenced your decision to become a writer?
I love Dr. Maya Angelou. The first novel that had an impact on my life was *I Know Why the Caged Bird*

***Sings*. I knew after reading that book, I wanted to tell stories as well, stories that had an impact on people. I also read a lot of contemporary authors including Jacqueline Thomas, Victoria Christopher Murray, Jihad, Eric Jerome Dickey, and a host of others.**

9. Why did you decide to include Hurricane Katrina in your story? Were you or people close to you directly affected by the storm?

   As a TV reporter for fifteen years, I've never covered a story that affected me like Hurricane Katrina. In all my years as a journalist, I've never shed a tear while covering a story until Katrina. It pained my heart to watch that devastation. Some of our friends ended up staying with us after the hurricane and their lives would never be the same. Donovan is actually inspired by a young athlete who was good enough to go pro directly from high school in New Orleans, but his life was completely uprooted after the hurricane. I'm happy to say that he is now playing college basketball.

10. In your own life, what has been the biggest blessing in disguise? What did it take for you to recognize the blessing?

    My mother. Growing up, my mother was strict. While all my friends could hang out until two in the morning, she wasn't having it. She even showed up at a club one time (in her hair rollers) when I missed curfew. I thought I would die of embarrassment and I absolutely couldn't stand my mom. What I didn't realize then that I do now was that was God's way of keeping me on track. He was working through my mother to make sure that I could become the woman I am today. I didn't realize it at the time, but my mother and all her strict rules was the biggest blessing I could have ever known.

Don't miss the next Good Girlz adventure

With Friends Like These

Coming in April 2007

Turn the page for a preview of *With Friends Like These* . . .

Camille

"My name is Tameka Adams and I don't want to be here." Tameka made the announcement like she was at an Alcoholics Anonymous meeting.

Personally, I wanted to tell her to beat it, then. I know one thing, if she was coming to join our group, homegirl was gon' have to lose the attitude. I mean, I know she's Rachel's niece by marriage and all. But her and her funky attitude needed to go.

Rachel is our group leader, the founder of the Good Girlz community service group. Don't let the name fool you, though. We all are far from good. Rachel started the group here in Houston as part of some youth outreach program at Zion Hill Missionary Baptist Church, where her husband was pastor. Her old snooty church members didn't want her to start the group. But even though she's First Lady, Rachel marches to a beat of her own. She told those old biddies where they could go. Now here we are, a year after we started. And even those people who didn't want us at first, are now feeling us.

I ain't gon' even lie, though, I came here kickin' and screamin'. But since my choice was either the Good Girlz or jail, well, I guess you could see why I'm here. The bad part was I got in a whole bunch of trouble over my stupid, no good, stank, dirty dog ex-boyfriend, Keith. Long story short, the fool went to jail for a carjacking, broke out and had me hiding him in my grandma's house. Then when the police came, he took off through a back window and I was the one who got arrested for harboring a fugitive. Can you believe that? Me, a straight A (well, sometimes B and C) person, got arrested. I was only fifteen so I didn't have to go to regular jail. I spent a week in a juvenile facility while they had a manhunt for Keith. And do you know where they found that dog? At his baby mama's house. That was a bit of a problem because I didn't know he had a baby. And I dang sure didn't know he had a baby mama.

Anyway, he got sent back to jail. They eventually found out he didn't do it—it was his stepbrother—so he got out. And of course, he tried to come running back to me but I wasn't hearing it. (Okay, maybe I did take him back one time, but he messed up again, cheating on me with his crazy baby mama, so I kicked him to the curb and I hadn't talked to him since.)

"Hello. Earth to Camille."

I looked up to see Angel waving her hand in my face.

I snapped back to the meeting, not even realizing my mind had wandered off.

"Glad you could rejoin us," Rachel said with a smile.

I shot her an apologetic look as she continued talking.

"Now that I've explained to our new girls all of the benefits of our wonderful group, we want everyone to introduce themselves," Rachel said. "Starting with you, Jasmine."

"Aww, Miss Rachel, it's not like Tameka doesn't know us. She's been here before," Jasmine protested. Tameka had come to our first meeting, but at the time, she chose not to participate. I don't know what had brought her back this time.

"It's not like she even wants to know us," I mumbled.

Rachel must've heard me because she cut her eyes at me. "Yes, but Jordan doesn't know everyone," Rachel said, referring to the brown-skinned girl sitting in the front row. "And why must you give me a hard time on everything?" Rachel asked Jasmine.

"Fine," Jasmine said. "I'm Jasmine Jones." She turned to Rachel with a huge smile. "How's that?"

Me, Alexis, and Angel cracked up laughing. Jasmine was our girl. She'd been like Tameka when we first started, a mean tomboy who didn't want to be here. But we'd broken down her guard and now she was totally cool. We are all tight. The only other person who'd been in our group was Alexis's friend, Trina. She joined for a little while, but got arrested for shoplifting and sent to jail. (That's another long story.) So I think none of us were too keen on anyone else joining our little circle, especially somebody with a funky attitude like Tameka.

Rachel rolled her eyes. "You all are working my nerves."

Alexis raised her hand. "I'll go, Miss Rachel. My name is Alexis Lansing," she said, standing up, tossing her long golden brown hair over her shoulder. "I'm a junior at St. Pius Catholic School."

"But she definitely ain't no Catholic schoolgirl," I playfully muttered, referring to her part in the little shoplifting spree she and Trina went on a few months ago. Angel high-fived me as Alexis, who was standing in front of me, shot me the finger behind her back.

"Big mouth over here is Camille Harris," Alexis continued, pointing to me. "And that is Angel Lopez," she said, pointing at Angel. "All of them are juniors at Madison High School."

Jordan gave us a smile. She was a weird-looking girl with long black hair that looked like it was in need of a good washing. She wore a long black skirt and long-sleeved black T-shirt, even though it was the middle of August.

"Now, Jordan, do you want to tell us a little about yourself?" Rachel asked.

Jordan shrugged. "Not much to tell. I go to Lamar High School and I had to come here because my friends do drugs. I don't, but my parents think I do because I hang around them. They think by my coming here, it'll cure me."

We all stared at her. That girl was a druggie if I ever seen one.

"Well, even though you don't think you need to be here, maybe you'll get something out of our group," Rachel said.

Jordan didn't look convinced. But Rachel didn't seem to notice as she began talking about all the community service projects we would be working on, including the one we had scheduled for Saturday.

By the time we wrapped up, I think all of us were worn out. Alexis, Angel, and Jasmine immediately gravitated toward each other, so I decided to personally welcome Jordan and Tameka, who were sitting off by themselves.

"Hey, are you guys going to be at the community service project Saturday?" I asked.

Tameka folded her arms and stuck out her bottom lip. "I guess, since it seems like we don't really have a choice."

Jordan rolled her eyes. "Not if I can help it."

The three of us stood there, looking around awkwardly. I noticed Angel, Alexis, and Jasmine cracking up about something. Finally, when I saw neither Jordan or Tameka were in a talkative mood, I shrugged. "Oh, well. See you guys later." I went back to my friends, telling myself I'd tried. I'd just stick to the original Good Girlz, the ones I knew were my true friends. I guess we just had no room for outsiders.

